Likheleke tsa puo

New Writing From Lesotho

Edited by Lineo Segoete, Makate Maieane and Zachary Rosen
Cover design by Zachary Rosen
Cover photograph by Lineo Segoete

ISBN: 978-0-9984513-0-5 | 978-0-9984513-1-2

Barelitfest.com | facebook.com/barelitfest

Contents

Editor's note

This year, we as the Ba re e ne re team, took on the massive responsibility of compiling a collection of short stories written by young Basotho. We wanted to demonstrate our recognition of the abundance of wonderful writers and fascinating stories in Lesotho and pay homage to the legacy set by our elders. The likes of Thomas Mokopu Mofolo, Mpho 'Mampeke Makara, LBBJ Machobane and many others set the bar by offering us long-form fiction writing that is as unique and potent as our poetry is. This compilation was a challenge to the current generation of writers to express their appreciation of language as an art form and show off their creativity. We also saw it as an opportunity to offer them a platform for their voices to be heard. The entire continent of Africa is reclaiming its stories and telling them from its perspectives and we are determined to be part of this renaissance. We are marking our presence because we too are active citizens building towards positive change and a vibrant future.

This book represents a great stride in setting the tone for what's to come. We hope it will inspire aspirant storytellers to have confidence and dare to take chances. There are so many things happening in our communities and lives that we need to cast light upon for our development and celebration. Gone are the days when it was ok to let outsiders control the narration of our realities. We have the power to shape how we are perceived and we can shine through stereotypes defined by those who view us as targets of scrutiny. We, Basotho, are fortunate enough to have a culture and history unlike many, and if we start looking closely enough we will all realise the wealth surrounding us. The written word is a powerful tool of communication that engages the senses, triggers the imagination and calls for critical thinking; qualities that are essential to learning and growth. Therefore, it is our mission as Ba re e ne re to promote, preserve and publish the written word's creative usage. We hope you enjoy this offering and that it makes you thirst for more.

Rea leboha!

Lineo Segoete
December 2016

Foreword

The value of creative writing provides a writer with an opportunity to articulate their own feelings or ideas, thereby moulding one's mind into organised and disciplined thinking. This process helps the writer to understand themself and succeed in connecting with their target audience. The passion to write must be encouraged to enable the writer's discipline and introspection, therefore, exercising people's minds at a young age to focus on improving these values remains critical.

This brings me to my late daughter Liepollo Rantekoa, the founder of the Ba re e ne re Literature Festival, who believed that young minds must be encouraged to identify within themselves the ability to appreciate their own creativity and to document and share their thoughts with a larger audience. She believed that young minds can learn and understand who they are, through early exposure to creative writing. From a very young age, Liepollo would demonstrate her feelings and observations through written notes to friends and family. She had the distinctive way of using words, which showcased her artistic and imaginary mind drawn from the heart. She enjoyed tapping into other people's thoughts and gauging the effect of her ideas on others by initiating discussions on topics of interest to her. Over the years, she dreamt of assisting young children to develop the reading habit to enhance their knowledge as she believed that "Knowledge is Power." She also believed that the reading habit and the celebration of literature will help awaken the sleeping giant of creative writing within the youth of Lesotho, hence the establishment of "BA RE E NE RE," its annual literature festival, and the dream of establishing reading centres in the rural areas within Lesotho. I am confident this book is going to change the face of history in Lesotho for many years to come by raising the level of enthusiasm for book writing from within the youth.

'Mantsane Rantekoa
December 2016

Lerato? Fokol!

Tšeliso Monaheng

"Ke sf'eng?": ke Pita Mokonyana eo ho kharebe ea hae Likhabiso.

"Ak'u bue le 'na hantle hle baybee, acheke!": ho arabela Likhabiso. "Ke u joetse hakae hore I don't like it ha u bua nyaft eo ea hau ho 'na?!"

Likhabiso o cho joalo, o bile o pasela ka ho tsunkanya sefahleho, a b'a itlhomolla 'atleng tsa Pita, a lula motšeo, thoko ho eena.

Pita, hona le hore a mamele Likhabiso, a utloe sello sa hae, a ikhethela ho potetsa letsoho la hae le letona 'thekeng la moeka, a mo hulela pel'a hae, a 'meha letlapahali la bo-nka-ntjana holim'a lerama le letšehali. Hotsoa ka hore na u botsa mang, Pita e ne 'le tlefa ea li-tlefa kapa koata ena e haesale!

"Mmmxwah!" ha tsanyaola molomo ho lerama. "Mmmmxwetenene!" oa pheta hape molomo oa Pita, eena molula-qhooa sebaka-manyofo-nyofo ntate!

Likhabiso o il'a leka ho iphapanya, a fapantša melomo, a b'a pasela ka ho famola linko, empa Pita bari ea litakana h'a ka ba mo tsotella. O il'a tsoela pele ho pholla atla sa Likhabiso, a b'a mo pasela ka ho mathisa seatla sefubeng moo matsoele a hlonngoeng seka lithaba li hana ho matahana a neng a nomorile teng ho bonahala eka a batla ho nyarela hore le 'ona a bone lietsahala.

Hose hokae, Likhabiso a iphumana mose, bothisi le mokoarela li se li le thoko koana, ha eena a n'a s'a nts'a le betheng.

"Baybee": o bitsa Pita, lentsoe la hae le e-na le ho thothomela ho sa tloalehang. "Baybee oe, not today. Taba ea last week ha ea ntula hantle so ke kopa re discuss-e ka eona instead."

Pita, ea neng a lutse holim'a k'heisi ea k'hotho a ntse a qetela ho fasolla lieta e le hore borikhoe bo lokolohe h'a bo hlobola, a se mo tsotelle.

Likhabiso: "Baybee oe!"

Pita a hlokomela hore kharebe ea hae ha ea lokoloha. Eaba o re: "Hao mfwethu, hakere ua tseba hore na ke sfeng ka taba tsa last week. Ska etsa nthoana nthohali, why u etsa so mareng?"

Hang, monahano oa Likhabiso oa boela maobanyana. Pita o n'a mo emelletse ka mokho'o bobe ba hae bo leng ka teng, bo keke ba pateha ho sa tsotellehe hore na o itlotsa ka pontše kae. A pasela ka moo eena a sa rateng ha Likhabiso a tsamaea le metsoalle ea hae ea lifebe kateng, le hore a keke a mo lumella ho tsoela kantle h'a ka ba 'n'a leka manyampetla a etsoang ke tjhomi tsa hae.

Empa tseo ha li buue hakere?! Joang ha mantsoe a mathe-maloli bo li *I love you* e le pheko ea mahlaba 'ohle?

"I love you."

Pita o bua mantsoe ao a s'a le mabapa le Likhabiso, a b'a pasela ka: "Ke u rata bolaente mfwethu." Senohe sena sa mohlankana se ne se se methile hore na o tsoela pele joang.

Likhabiso eena sefuba se ne se kanna sa phatloha kamoo a neng a hemesela kateng. Pelo e n'e otla ka sekhahla se phahameng hoo u neng u ka nahana hore hona le bokulo bo mo tšoereng.

Ho hema hona hone ho bakoa ke takatso, tlholohelo le taba-tabelo ea tlalo la Pita holim'a la hae, hammoho le letsoalo la hore na ho bolel'ang ho itumella ho tšoareha maikutlo ka monna ea mo joetsitseng mantsoe a bohloko, a mo petsotseng pelo ka makhetlohali.

"Baybee. Baybee oe! Ke kopa u emise..."

*

Likhabiso Janki e n'e le moroetsan'a Saofo koana motsaneng o bitsoang Nka-u-betsa-ke-u-phete, porofinsing ea Molia-Nyeoe. Moren'a baka seo e e n'e le monn'a morutehi ea bitsoang Terantala, ea ileng a ba lehlohonolo la ho tsoellisa lithuto tsa hae pele kamor'a ho fuoa lisentjana ke 'muso oa naha tlas'a lekala la bona la Matla-A-Monna.

Marang-rang a khokahanyo a n'a bapala bana motseng oa morena eo. Maseea a ntseng a hloephetsa mamina a na nyafa li-bantlele joalokaha moja-mahe a khoatha mayonnaise. Internet e n'e le boieane, khokahanyo e matha ho elelleng li-kika-bytseng koana. Bo li-YouTube le oebsaet tse ling tsa maemo e n'e le ti-ti, pote! Hosena manyampetla ana ao motho a tlamehang ho ema letsatsi kaofela hore taonloutu e qete. Baahi ba Nka-u-betsa ba ne ba hafa ka nkatana!

Likhabiso o il'a hlalefa kapele ke hona.

E n'e le e mong oa batho ba pele ba ho ba le leqephe la Myspace profinsing. Li-hashtag li fihla e le hore moeka e s'e le sekoankoetla sa marang-rang a khokahanyo. O tsebile esale khale hore eena h'a fihla Junfesithi o tl'o ithutela ho ba setsebi se hloahloa sa Likomporo.

O n'a tseba lintho li se kae ka thobalano. O n'a sa tsebe hore o tla kopana le Pita; hore e tla ba eena mohlankana oa pele oa ho mo hlekefetsa.

Pita o n'a sa mamele. Le lapeng habo e n'e le ntho e tloaelehileng. E n'e tla re ha nkhon'ae a re hona, eena a re hoane. 'M'ae o n'a sebetsa hole Makichineng a Makhooa, ntat'ae eena esale a ipha naha. Ke hona, Pita o n'a ikutloa bokoankoetla, a ipona e le sehanyatha se ka nkang mosali-moholo sa mo hleka tseleng ka potlako.

Sephiri se ne se ipatse eena.

"Baybee, not today hle..."

Likhabiso o bua joalo e le hore ho chang hoane ho ikeme ka ho fetjha. Ho eena, e n'e le toka hore haeba kharebe e bontšitse takatso e holimo ea nama, ebile e u lumelletse hore u e hlobolise, ke tokelo ea hau joalo'ka monna hore u tsoele pele u qetele seo u se qalileng.

A tsoela pele ke hona. Likhabiso lentsoe ea ka lea cha. Ho hema ha kopana le ho tsetsela; le likhapha; le mamina. Pelo eona tlepe! Ka har'a malana. A utloa eka a ka kopa hore lefaatše le mo kometse a tl'a tsebe ho nyamele kapele, ka potlako.

Praying Wives' Club

Refiloe Mabejane

Strolling down the corrugated iron-shacked passages of Stopong to 'Mae's office in the part of town where it's easier to breathe, I already know what to expect. I will sit in a corner by the window overlooking the Queen II hospital mortuary across the rutted tar street. I never ever see a corpse from there no matter how long I stare, so I always end up on the floor, scribbling on the endless white paper pads with the gold Lesotho coat of arms. 'Mae and I will later join the other civil servants on the half past four march to the jam I am in now, past Maseru Central Park which is opposite the Pentecostal church, where tired home wreckers go, she always says, to buy new identities from a clever pastor. The queue for the 4+1 taxi to Khubetsoana will salute us after we soldier the hill past the Chinese shop, known as Good or Best Supermarket, the one I just passed and yet still can't say which it is.

That's what always happens when I am removed from class like I have been each year since he left, and that's what I am expecting when I finally walk into 'Mae's glass cubicle after my fun trips up and down the elevator. The air is vinegary, from the chips she often buys from the shop downstairs, though she always complains that they are fried in the same oil over and over. She almost jumps out of her chair, eyes popping like they never saw the usual warning letters, like the one I brought home a week before. The letter declared, in far from uncertain terms, in Times New Roman, my name curled in blue ink in the belly of the page, that if the fees were not paid on the something[th] of January, I would be taken out of class. The only thing we had never seen before was the date.

"Is it the fees?" 'Mae still asks.

"Yes. They sent me out of class at 9, but Mrs. Molikeng said I couldn't leave school until the end of the day. I just left. I'm tired, you know. The other kids laugh at me when they come out for break!"

"Yes my child, you did well. I'll speak to them. I don't understand why they want you to stay outside like a hobo. I must also speak to Leeto about the fees. I only managed to pay for your brother. Please understand Meme, high school is more serious than primary." The words shoot out of her mouth like bullets from a gun, her big eyes hula hooping.

My brother does need the fees more; he's the one who was tossed to boarding school. Sometimes I wonder if it was punishment for looking like our father, maybe 'Mae couldn't bear to look at his face more than during school breaks, or maybe she trusted the men at the boys-only school to raise him better. For me, if not for the embarrassment of being removed from class, to everyone's amusement, I don't care about not being in school. No matter how long I stay home, which I enjoy because I get to read books that are not schoolbooks, I am always in the Top 2. By the time she is able to patch together the fees, I hate having to break my reading, eating, reading, eating and reading routine.

Today is not going to be just another day to doodle behind 'Mae's small desk. She tells me it is a Praying Wives' Wednesday. I follow her thick frame down the corridor, irritated that there is no need for the elevator because the meeting hall with once cream, now browning walls is on the same floor as her office. A rabbit-faced, praying wife with elephant legs sits on the only chair in the room, rising to fuss about as we enter. I am walking behind 'Mae so I can get away with just mumbling as she greets, but this woman lunges at me, patting my afro. I look down to hide my annoyance, and she wheels a black swivel chair into a corner for me to sit on, saying, "No problem 'M'e, anyway it's never too early for them to learn," because 'Mae is busy apologising for my being here.

12

More Praying Wives stroll into the room. Rabbit Face moves to the front of the hall and breaks into their murmurs with a velvety voice that stops the women's chatter. She, like someone who has no idea how good she sounds, lightly slaps the black hardcover of her pink-mouthed bible as she sings, "Tsela e thata joang, o re e tsamaeang, leeto le tla feela re kene Kanana!" How difficult the road we travel, but the journey will end and we will get to Canaan. As they join in the melody, the women sway from side-to-side rhythmically as if to signify some sort of glory in suffering.

Rabbit Face moves into prayer thanking God for the safe holiday season, and "giving us the space and the minutes, to come together," because he said, "where two or three gather in my name, I too will be there." So she begs him to be there with them and to send the Holy Spirit to guide their talks for the day so that they may leave uplifted. I don't dare ask, but, if God himself is here already, do they still need to bother with Holy Spirit?

"I'll go first," says a small-built Praying Wife with a mole on her pointy nose. She grips the edges of her grey suit jacket together unaffectedly. "Over December I continued practicing what bo-'M'e taught me." Her replacement of the c in "December" with a z stings my ears; in class you get five lashes from Mrs. Mohajane for that. "And the fruits show. Our home is happier. It is quieter. When he comes home at 5am, I don't confront him. I just help him undress, and then he's dead. They are truly like children – these men. So when he wakes up, we still have our peace. My anger is what made him angry, and giving up the anger has worked so well, not like when I would shout at him and he would be in a bad mood all weekend."

"Did you use the water trick?" asks one Praying Wife with an upper body like The Rock of WWE, but a lower body not much bigger than mine, stroking the pearly rosary on her black haired, yellow arm.

"No, I just kept replaying bo-'M'e's words in my head. Humble yourself, humble yourself, I kept telling myself, submit. I mumbled it every time I walked back from opening the door for him." Dezember's lips move more than I have ever seen any pair of lips move in my life, with two painful-looking bumps forming between her eyebrows as she speaks.

Sitting like a terrorist avoiding detection, with only my eyes moving over the women planted on the thinning maroon carpet, I suddenly wish that they were rather moving over pages of the *Things Fall Apart* I left under my pillow at home. As I study the tall, light-skinned, medium height, brown-skinned women, they seem to have nothing in common, nothing special, as women whose husbands need praying for. Nothing except maybe that they are all – including 'Mae – wearing gold wedding rings, and whenever they talk, they all use the ring hands to gesticulate.

The next Praying Wife to speak has a voice so deep that before I see her curvaceous figure, I think that for sure a Praying Husband has snuck in.

"For me, it is the water thing that has worked. Before, I used to always go to the window to check if every sound was his car pulling into the yard. Now that I have learnt to inject myself with the peace that the word of God gives me, I sleep until I'm awoken by his knocking, whenever he decides to come home." It always surprises me when a very pretty woman - with skin as beautiful as I always imagined the girls in my novels to have - speaks with a coarse voice. "But because I know I may be tempted to break the rules and shout about where he has been, I always go to the kitchen and take some water. It really helps because sometimes I know without the water in my mouth reminding me to keep quiet, I would lose control."

"That's great my sister, because where your husband has been, and with whom, is none of your business. Ephesians 22 only asks the husband to love the wife. The wife's job is to respect the husband. Men are few and we are many my sisters, so let's just be grateful when they come home. Some leave never to return! Remember that

14

when he enters your house, there is someone out there wishing he was entering hers." It was The Rock again. "Men don't like all the barking in their ears that we used to do, even if he has come home late. You must thank God he didn't leave then, before you learned submissiveness! And if he wants you at whatever hour he comes to you, give it to him, give him all of it! You know marriage is the lottery. What you don't give him, there are others waiting out there to give him!" I wonder if she would speak so freely about "it" if she knew "it" isn't much of a code for an eleven-year-old.

I have decided The Rock is their leader. She doesn't have the others' carefulness. She speaks bravely like teachers, like people who are to be listened to and not advised. I knew 'Mae liked to say they were equal, but even teachers like to claim you can tell them if they're wrong, though you know they are just saying it. Indeed she is their leader, the master of respecting a man who doesn't respect her or himself. I once heard my mother talk of how The Rock's own husband lives at a shebeen.

"For me the Praying Wives Club has helped me understand that refusing my husband chips will only make him go more to other women. Now, I am ever-ready," says the light skinned one with two huge mountains on her chest, uttering the last word with a smile of many meanings I wouldn't expect from a Praying Wife. "I only know of one girl now, and it doesn't bother me because they do it with respect. He is still giving me money, and love, and she does not bother me like some mistresses bother us. When I see her at the mall I don't even look at her." I try to think about how "chips" came to mean what I think it does, but then here is The Rock's voice again, over which no thinking can happen.

"And as we've learnt through seeking comfort in the word, the bible only asks husbands to love their wives, so as long as he still loves you, what would you be crying about?" The Rock doesn't say this like it is a question and no one answers. They seem to silently swallow the words spat into their mouths like infant birds, like 'Mae has swallowed their every word, ever since joining them some months before her own husband's silent departure from the house. *As long as I remember to play my role and to respect my husband, God will work in our lives,* had stolen her heart, and her sanity. *He doesn't know what he is doing. Men are weak. He is just lost. God will bring him back to me.* Even before Ntate had left, 'Mae spoke again and again of the coming back. I hadn't quite understood until he actually left us, taking with him a chunk of her mind.

'Mae had been inside her own bowed head the whole time, only looking up sometimes or nodding. Now she is speaking, trembling, her cornrowed head tilted to one side, "As you can see, this child here, she is not at school, her fees have not been paid because I don't know a cent of his money and I am struggling to do things with the nothing you know I earn here. But I am staying strong bo-'M'e, praying to the Virgin Mary because where else can I run but to my mother? She will feel my pain and evaporate the muti that the witch used on my husband." It makes me want to crawl under the chair hearing 'Mae say the man who is living happily with another woman is her husband. She repeats it, "My husband's eyes will open when it evaporates, and he will come back. I will be waiting with open arms because in the eyes of the church that married us, we are still husband and wife! Yes he's still my husband because as we all know, in God's house there's no divorce!" She almost sings that last sentence, finger dancing in the air. Ntate has been gone for three years.

Maybe it's because she wasn't there that day. He didn't look like Ntate at all in his faded jeans and golf shirt with its collar "popped." He looked like a boy. His look reminded me of his son's look the day 'Mae caught him playing with his thing. She dove for the holy water and started sprinkling it all over his body with her hands as he lay in his check boxer shorts, tongue fastened by shame, in the middle of his single bed. She spat, "Get out of my son, Satan, out! Out! Out! Out!

16

"Where is 'Matseleng? This must be the fourth Wednesday she's missing?" The Rock roars, throwing her brown bag over her broad shoulder. Were he here, that brother of mine would have called the bag's leather-like material "me I peel" before lunging into lengthened laughter.

"'Matseleng is not coming. I met her at Shoprite on Sunday. She was wearing leggings and you could see she hadn't even been to church at all, my God! She told me that she wasn't coming back to this group," replied the Praying Wife with a voice like a Praying Husband whom I have decided is the prettiest, though I can't be trusted, because Ntate always said I have "a strange eye." Would Ntate and his friends, Ntate Mokoatle and Ntate Thamae, and some of the other men he knows, ever meet to make each other good husbands? I don't dare ask.

"'M'e, she is divorcing. She moved out of the house. She left her man," the woman's shoulders droop as if heavy with the other woman's sin.

"Oh Mary Mother of God! 'Matseleng thinks she can compete with a man? Oh Virgin Mary! What are we going to do? A woman can't do what a man does. If he finds out he'll never forgive you, he'll leave you!" The Rock is fuming, the "me I peel" thumping as it drops to the floor. She fires on like she did not hear the bag fall. "We are not men, bo 'M'e! A man is a pumpkin, he spreads out – but a woman, bo-'M'e, a woman must always contain herself like a cabbage. A woman must pray for her husband, her family. Our place is on our knees! Ours is not revenge!"

The women in our village always say about 'Matseleng, "it is like she has never given birth that one," because of her fit body and upright breasts. One Christmas a group of us went to her house to ask for "a Christmas" like children in the village do every year. She gave us a whole pack of chocolate sweets, something we had never got from any other house before. She was wearing yellow and pink striped

Pyjama shorts with a pink tank top, her long hair hanging on her shoulders. She was nothing like 'Mae, who, ever since I could remember, slept in a sagging flowery nightdress with a brown pantyhose covering her head; nothing like, 'Mae whose hair never seemed to be that black or grow that long anyway, whose breasts lay limp on her chest like the battered bodies on medical reality shows.

The Rock is still at it.

"When God finally answers her prayers and her husband comes back home and says sorry, she does this? All men are the same, what are you going to gain from jumping from one to the next? A Mosotho woman doesn't behave like that, she's bewitched I swear! What will her children say, a woman that old bumping into walls like that? Ah, my sisters, this world needs prayer. Women are no longer the women God planned for us to be." She ends with a weary sigh, "Let's pray bo-'M'e. We have gone over the lunch hour."

'Mae cuts in with the voice, a voice desperate to move closer to heaven, a voice that convinces me there really is a praying voice for when we speak to God. No one seems to speak to Him as we speak to each other here on earth, from the way we mend our voices, to the way faces go into a deep, deep daze. Yet, as 'Mae begins, I cannot stop from thinking that when my mother prays, God does other things, like a person who pretends to be listening as you rant, but is actually already imagining how they will tell your story to their peers later.

"We thank you father for this wonderful day that you have yet again given us. We thank you that you are sending the Holy Spirit to anoint us with submissiveness every week, to protect us from going outside the house like loose women. We thank you that in you we have found the strength to forgive our husbands, who are weaker than us, and easily tempted," she pauses, unclenching her fists and grandly placing one hand on her belly and the ring hand over it. Could 'Mae be thinking of something to say to God that will impress The Rock? I don't dare ask. "Thank you that we know we can never stray. I would particularly like to pray for our sister 'Matseleng, that she may be pulled out of the darkness into the light and see it is wrong to seek to take revenge on her husband because you God, have built us differently from men. Help us never think of ourselves as equal to our husbands, as it is for us to be under them. May we continue to become better women every time we meet. May this be a blessed year of seeing God's work in our lives and in our families."

When we walk through our wobbly wire and wood gate I am still thinking how the only thing I learnt in there was that I never want to be a Praying Wife, a woman who says "God's work" when she means the return of a man who clearly doesn't want to come back. Our washing lady 'Malerato meets us at the kitchen door. She has to have been peeking through the window because she opens before we can even knock. My first thought is why she isn't watching *The Bold and the Beautiful*. Then I catch the look on her face. It is like the one she had one afternoon when she got a call to say her daughter's baby had been delivered on the long walk to hospital.

"'M'e 'Malebeko," she says my mother's name five more times while leading us to the sitting room where Rangoane, my father's brother, is sitting with his legs so far apart it is a wonder his tight shiny pants remain intact. What looks like it did come apart and was quickly put together as we entered is his face.

"Hei Bafokeng," he muttered our family totem about as many times as 'Malerato had just said my mother's name.

Ntate returned, two weeks from that day. He returned in a mahogany casket that was part of his Plan A funeral policy, one of the papers on which he and 'Mae were still together. All that waiting and condemning women who wear leggings and leave husbands, all that praying for his eyes to open, and Ntate came back, his eyes forever shut. The woman he loved had left him, while the woman who was his wife in her head prayed for him to leave her. Whilst the woman he did

19

not love prayed, Ntate roped his neck to a garage roof and all she got was a spot on the mourning mattress before the funeral and a black everyday dress for four months after. 'Mae was lucky because at least he died in January, or she would have been blackened for a whole year.

Everything is Relative

Pontšo Mpholle

As the yellow, oil-leaking bus coughs its way out of the bus stop, my mother waves frantically, gushing with pride at my jolt into independence, but equally dreading my leaving. I wave back and smile, stifling a riot of tears which are burning the interior of my eyelids and I realise how much I will miss her. Tied around her waist is a green and white cloth with tessellating patterns. It matches the one wrapped around her head. Tucked inside the waist cloth is a grey, worn out 'Know your status' t-shirt. The t-shirts are free to those who test for HIV at the local clinic, but some people shamelessly exploit that goodwill for a free t-shirt every now and again.

My mother's face is a map of hardships, but the kindness in her big, brown eyes masks any past troubles. The kindness is as prominent as the *M* which parts her lips. Traces of ancient beauty still linger on her sagging face; high cheekbones, a faint sparkle in her eyes and outwardly curved lips. I watch her wave until the bus leaps onto the tar road perforated with potholes and slithers behind a row of trees.

The bus, which is full to the brim, is a hive of activity. Some unlucky passengers will have to stand the entire journey. It's the nature of things; there are always those that have to stand. I can only imagine the muscle stiffness that shall ensue. Beside me is an old man who succumbed to sleep immediately after planting himself on the seat. A woman and her wildly crying baby sit across from us. The baby cries relentlessly and she tries to calm him. I catch a glint of exasperation flashing in her eyes. I come to think that the child must be ill. The woman then slaps out her deflated, black breast with its wrinkled nipple and tries to pacify the child, but he spits it out in protest and continues his barbaric screams.

Somewhere at the front, a man I cannot see is preaching about the end of the world. He is so impassioned in his speech that I imagine he must be sticking his elbows in people's faces, causing them to curse him so vilely that they dare not egress the words from their lips for fear that the Lord might strike them down.

"Repent now brothers and sisters, for the end of days is nigh," he shouts above the noise in the bus.

I see someone discreetly chuck a crumpled piece of paper out of the window. It is one of the pamphlets the preacher is distributing in his quest to relay and support his Armageddon warning, hoping that the illustrations of vicious tongues of fire springing from the imagined abyss of hell will drive the point home. I don't believe him but I try to listen anyway.

The stuffiness in the bus mixed with fetid odours of perspiration and rotting food scattered somewhere on the floor begins to irritate me. The crying baby has quieted a bit and I am as relieved as the mother. I stretch my arms over my head to ease my growing stiffness, taking deep breaths as I do so. An hour has passed since we departed and the atmosphere is thick with colourful chatter and roars of laughter. I keep expecting the bus to break down, but it spites me by continuing its tailpipe bronchitis all the way to the beckoning city.

Looking outside I start to wonder: What are all these people going to do in the city? Perhaps some are visiting relatives; aunts and uncles and cousins. Others may have errands to run for this one day only, likely bulk grocery shopping because the village shops are ridiculously overpriced. But others, like me, look like they don't plan to return. They are dream-chasers hoping to find a better life in the city, or the closest illusion to it.

We, from the villages, always hear stories about the teeming opportunities in the city. When they return from the city, some villagers appear so gleaming of riches that you'd swear cows shoot rainbows out of their asses and shit money there. For those eluded by the proverbial better life, they end up filling the piss-stained streets and aggravating the population of rats and humans alike, the shame too great to allow them to return home. That too, is the nature of things.

Three hours after leaving my rural village I arrive in the city, my buttocks aching and ears buzzing. A crowd of people are moving in all directions busying themselves like ants foraging for food. Vendors with their assortment of goods wave them excitedly and accost us when we get off the bus. One burly woman shoves a sachet of something in my face, which she guarantees will enlarge my breasts. I shake my head reluctantly. I am sixteen - they will grow naturally. However, the woman on the bus with the crying baby may need the dubious thing in the packet.

***

I slowly drag my fingers over my face and pause to inspect the scatter of pigmentation spots on my cheeks and the persistent dark circles beneath my eyes. A small, newly-formed pimple on my temple distracts me for a while and I tamper with it trying to pop it. Popping will only worsen it, this I know, but defiance guides my fingertips as they press feverishly against the puss-saturated bump. My hands deftly search my face like those of a blind man, traversing my nose and sliding over my full lips.

Somehow the crack along the length of the my handheld mirror has stopped bothering me and I have learned to ignore it. Like one does to a frenzied fly. I recall in fragments that one night when I was terribly drunk and awoke in my room to a half-shattered mirror strewn amongst toppled chairs and an overturned table. But it couldn't have been me who was the hurricane because I remember Thabo yelling and cursing about something which my brain failed to decipher. Now, looking into the mirror, my reflection has an oblique crack across it, meandering down from my hairline to my left cheek, resembling those on my village councilmen's faces; (the two-faced bastards!).

My panties need to be replaced, I think to myself as I rummage through a messy shelf which I always postpone cleaning because I have duly mastered the art of procrastination. They are beginning to wear at the seams and the colours are fading. My hand explores further and gets entangled by a necklace I stole at Sefika Complex, in a fancy boutique where I obviously did not belong. I ambled in there one hot summer's day fanning my face, feigning an 'English medium school' accent and dazzled the saleslady with my expertly forged sophistication.

I had gotten a hefty tip the previous night so I washed myself up really nicely and bought some cheap perfume, new heels, and a counterfeit Louis Vuitton handbag. It was so identical to the real thing that even I wasn't convinced it was a knock-off. The saleslady went into a welcoming frenzy when I walked in. She must have done that a lot. I snuck the diamond necklace inside my sham handbag whilst she was reaching for a fascinator I had no interest in buying, but raved about and narrated lies of how I had bought a similar one in Cape Town.

I gaze back into the mirror and slap on a thick layer of foundation and blend it vigourously into my skin until the freckles have disappeared, then I slide a deep fuchsia lipstick over the lips, line my eyelids heavily with a black kohl pencil and flick on so much mascara that my lashes look artificial. The sudden detachment from basicness grows as I stare into the mirror, studying my face and how my cheekbones protrude like anthills. "Beautiful," I murmur, "maybe with a bit more powder," and I dab on some more. The cosmetics are the cheap Chinese kind that don't stay on for too long and the lipstick has to be re-applied every half-hour or so. I smile awkwardly to reveal a set of perfectly aligned but slightly yellowing teeth. Blame it on the cigarettes. Life here often gets my nerves into such a convoluted tangle that I seek solace in a ciggy or two or three. And lastly I spritz on that cheap perfume which has an aggressive floral scent that stings the nostrils if worn excessively.

***

"Take off your clothes," he says, in a husky authoritative voice and I assume that he must hold some managerial position at work. I oblige and slip out of my bright, orange mini-skirt with tasselled pockets, then off comes the crop top, which had exposed a network of jutting ribs. Only my matching sky-blue panty and bra with purple lace trimmings remain on my skinny frame as I sway slightly, grinding my hips from side to side. "Come here," he demands. I smile. Impressing him is absolutely crucial and I dare not fuck this up. The young girl who endured a long, uncomfortable bus journey to the city five years back is long gone and in her place is a woman; now robustly feminine, but sadly transformed into one before she could barely fathom the attention she aroused from the boys in the village. His big, strong arms lay me against the white sheets and he strokes my chin sensually. He's a handsome man with beautiful features like the exquisite, black BMW M3 he parked beside me earlier in the night.

Being a prostitute is good money, better than most menial jobs in this city. I can afford rent for the squalid flat I occasionally share with mice and can keep my stomach invariably filled. But I didn't come to this city to prostitute myself to random men. I didn't choose this lifestyle, none of us ever does. When I came to the city I had big, but now seemingly outrageous hopes; to find a decent - and I use this term loosely – job, and to provide for my aging mother. That's all. However, life is like one big prank show and it enjoys throwing in soap operaesque twists for its amusement. Things didn't pan out as expected so here I am in a lavish hotel room with a stranger thrusting madly between my thighs.

I watch him as he dresses, paying attention to his well-built upper body. My eyes trail down to the intricate design of the tribal tattoo on his fore-arm and I instantly forget about Thabo as I relish this sight. Thabo is a total nuisance, but I have convinced myself that I love him. Not too many men show interest in women like me. They'd actually rather spit at, curse and humiliate us than show any sort of affection, so we take what we can get. Love - or some skewed semblance of it - for us, is like spoiled leftovers. We neatly remove the bits covered with mould and salvage what's left. I've learnt to love Thabo, I suppose. Apart from his job as a welder, he is also a full-time alcoholic and part-time womaniser. A typical man in this city.

My client puts on his black suit jacket and extracts a fat, tan leather wallet from the pants pocket. He's not much of a talker and all I hear from him is a sigh, just one, (a typical wussy-husband-succumbing-to-guilt sigh. I've heard a lot of these). After counting several notes, he puts them on the side table. "There's your money," he says and leaves without even a look in my direction. I don't know why, but I feel somewhat bothered by that. Like a ghost, his cologne lingers - thankfully nostril-friendlier than my poltergeist of a fragrance - and seduces my senses as I reach for the pile of cash. He has left M500. To ensure that my eyes are being wholly truthful to me, I count the money about ten times, stacking and re-stacking the notes like a bank teller. I usually charge around M40 and this is much more than what I make on a decent night. This goes far beyond tipping. He might as well have purchased me entirely. I shriek with excitement, and throw the money into the air, watching it rain down on me like good fortune, the notes tickling my bare skin.

***

"Losing oneself is temporary," my father would say, "maintaining oneself is forever." I never fully understood those words until now, here, in this wretched city where snakes could easily be mistaken for people. Ntate was a wise man. He had a metaphysical understanding for everything, believing that our fates are culminations of little, yet overlooked happenings. I'd sit on his lap when I was little and he would tell me many fascinating folk tales. Being an only child meant that I always had his attention and so I hogged it all, leaving just enough for my mother. Although uneducated, my father was hard-working and motivated. He was a simple farmer of simple tastes.

I remember the day my father was murdered. It was on a Thursday. A hot Thursday. I'd splayed myself under the shade of a peach tree that afternoon, just waiting for the sun to duck behind the hills and be gone. The heat had me spent and sweat seeped into my clothes, creating a wonderful sensation when a stray breeze blew against my skin. The heaviness in my heart felt like there had been a big collision between two enormous celestial bodies, so great as to cause absolute extinction; so that no bird ever chirped again and morning dew never glistened on expectant leaves - so that life and the simple beauty of it ceased to exist. I was eleven at the time and I remember how I cried until I'd given myself a searing headache.

The thing about life is that when it fucks you over, even if there's prior warning, the impact is devastating. Overpowered by the violence, you are then left to curl up, arms shielding your head as you let your mind drift to faraway places whilst you wait for the assault by life to end. Your thoughts dart randomly from the itch on your scalp to your preference in fruit to your mother's many admonishments.

I watched helplessly as the assailants hacked my father to death with machetes, blood splattering everywhere like how juice squirts from a grape when you pop it. The man who'd locked me in his arms to restrain me tightened the more I wriggled, growling in my ear like a riled dog, most likely foaming at the mouth too. The onslaught continued and the weapons dove and rose in unison. It was as if they had rehearsed the whole thing, perfected it for months, envisioned the exact style by which they would kill him. An intense tug in my stomach triggered a shower of vomit which splashed over the restraining man's shoes. He slapped me so hard that I crashed jaw first into the ground. I cried loudly as the pain registered somewhere deep inside my brain. The ferocious pain spread rapidly across my face, leaving anguish in its wake. Mr. Restrainer lifted me roughly and mouthed insults about my mother's genitals, but all I could hear was the throb in my uncomfortably hot face.

Ntate stopped screaming - he was dead. Murmuring some incantations I could not make sense of the killers gathered his parts and threw them into a burlap sack, leaving his head exposed, and then signalled to the man holding me to release me. I rushed to Ntate's lifeless body - the little of it they were courteous enough to leave - ignoring the jelly-like feeling in my legs and the Ritcher Scale-10 earthquake of aching in my jaw. For what seemed like forever, I lay there absolutely numb, an insignificant speck of dust in the vast cosmos. I felt my insides crumble slowly as I caressed his powder white face. My mouth was dry and tears made it taste of salt - and heartache. I just sat there cupping his severed head in my hands. His blood pooled around me from gushing vessels and soaked into my pink, frilly dress.

***

I hate slow nights. The ones where merely getting three clients is a luxury. Slow nights usually amount to the survival of the most visually appealing. But different men have different tastes, you know. Some like bones and some prefer meat on the bones. Not even the most vulgarly exposed flesh can lure a client if he's certain about his preference. As the night wanes, I feel like I've wasted this new matching panty-bra set. Clients are few and far between and they all seem to be craving meat. Bones like myself are left competing to the death.

By the time the clock strikes midnight, I am exhausted from parading myself on the filthy pavement. It is crusty and stinky, probably from some drunkard's vomit. Every now and then I flick my DIY-ombre weave and bat my lashes at a potential client, but that's not enough for me to get picked. I remember how I struggled when I joined Suzie's turf. Wasn't just me though. All the newbies struggle in someone else's turf, not because of their obvious inexperience but rather because the dames, the older, more skilled women who control of the turf, are generally not easy-going. Suzie is brutal and doesn't tolerate nonsense. She is a chunky, 30-something, large-breasted woman with a personality as big as her bust.

"You're a bony one; that will mean more effort," she'd said with her raspy voice on my first night.

I reckon her voice is like that because of all the beer she downs. She is a borderline alcoholic, but none of us is brave enough to confront her about it so we usually entertain her drunken shenanigans. Suzie has two children, boys. Liteboho is twelve and Tieho is ten. The boys are what Suzie calls 'workplace accidents.' Although she doesn't know who their fathers are, she has told them that he - yes, only one - died in a car accident after Tieho was born, and convinced Liteboho that he was too young to remember. Other than that big, fat lie, she is a wonderful mother, contrary to what the social services people claimed when they attempted to take the children away from her.

***

I share this rundown flat with Thabo on days when he makes himself available to me, after he has passed through some Thato, Palesa and Lerato. I only like it because of its balcony. I take in the tobacco and the city, doused in a constellation of bright lights, with equal enthusiasm. On the balcony I get to reflect on the confusion of my life as the vibrance of the city soothes my soul and I lose myself to the trance of its poetic beauty.

Standing on the balcony I light a ciggy. I killed a man once. He was dark, tallish and had an unpleasant musty odour. I bashed him in the face with a brick several times. He was the cheap type that never booked a hotel room; the quickie-in-an-alley type. The cheeky bastard refused to pay me. We got into a scuffle. I was disadvantaged by his strength and fell down. Somewhere beneath all that frugality was the swollen nerve to call my mother a whore. I rose up slowly, livid and frothing but remained very silent, reached for a brick and bashed him behind the head. As soon as he turned around I sank the brick into his face. I think I broke his nose because I heard a loud crack. He screamed and pleaded for his life as he collapsed. But I just kept digging into him until he fell silent. I just left him there. The same way they'd left my father.

Liatla tsa motsoa-ntle

Mamoholi C. Mokhoro

Nakong eo lemati le bulehang, Motebang ha'ka tsotella ho phahamisa hlooho. 'Nete ke hore o ne a lebelletse Pokanelo. Motebang o ile a tsoelapele ho bapala ka mohala oa hae oa thekeng. Nakong eo a phahamisang hlooho, Pokanelo o ne a eme pel'a hae a mo shebile a thotse. Motebang o ile a otloa ke letsoalo habohloko hobane ho latela liketsahalo tsa matsatsi a 'maloa a pele ho moo, tebello ea hae e ne e le ea hore o tla bona Pokanelo a thohothetsoe, a hloentse, linko li kopane le phatla. Empa ka lebaka la ho ela ha sefahleho sa Pokanelo le bonolo ba sona, Motebang o ile a utloa a sehoa ke letsoalo lekhetlo la pele haesale a lula le eena, a ba a utloa eka ho na le ho itseng qapi! borikhoaneng ba hae ba ka hare.

Pokanelo o fihlile ho eena a theotse moea eka haho letho le etsahetseng. O ne a iphapantse hobane a hlokometse hore o ne a lula le sekoeta. Ka morao hore a bone na Motebang o fumana chelete ea hae joang, phoso ea hae e ne e be ho bua eaba o e jela ka letlalo. Lekhetlong lena Pokanelo o ne a se a ithutile hoba bohlale. Sepheo sa hae e ne e le ho khutlela hae a ntse a phela.

*

Ka letsatsi le leng Pokanelo Mothabeng o ne a tsamaea a feta lebenkeleng le leholo la Litholoana le Meroho har'a mp'a motšeare ka hare ho teropo ea Maseru. O ne a tsoa sekolong 'me a ea a lebile lebenkeleng le rekisang litšebeletso tsa marang-rang le ho alimisana libuka. O ile a panya hanyenyane feela a sheba ka nqa ho tsela e kholo ea likoloi eaba ka ona motsotso ono oa khoptjoa, a khothometseha ha bohloko, a ba a batla a ea fatše ka sanketse.

Ha a ka a qetella a oele. Ha a re etlo! O ile a iphumane a maname holim'a lipeta tsa monna eo a sa mo tsebeng ka har'a keribae. Ho latela tsela eo monna eo a neng a itšoarellelitse ka eona keribaeng moo, ho ne ho bonahala hore Pokanelo o ile a imamarella ka eena a sa elelloa, 'me ba oela 'moho. Moo Pokanelo le monna eo ba ntseng ba tjamellane eka ba tsoha torong ea mohlolo, mong'a keribae o ne a ntse a akha matsoho a re: "he *khotman*, emang *da*. U nsenyetsa nako, ke *spaneng da*."

Ba babeli bano ba ne ba thotse, ba shebane ka mahlong. Ba phaphame ha ba se ba tsosoa ke litlatse le mehoo ea sechaba se neng se se se ba teetse hare. Hang hoba ba eme monga keribae a e fofela hang-hang, a e fafola, a ba a potela a sa hetle.

"Ha u motsoala empa ke batla ho bitsa malito." Monna eo o ne a bua a bososela a otlollotse letsoho la hae ho Pokanelo. "Ke reiloe Motebang haeso, 'me nka thabela ho tsebana le ausi enoa e motle ea akhetsoeng ka hare ho liatla tsa'ka."

Pokanelo o ile a otlolla letsoho la hae le eena eaba o re: "*hi*! Ke Pokanelo. Ke kopa u ntšoarele, ke ne ke sa hlokomele hore hona le bohato bo phahameng ka pela'ka, joale ke hatile ke sa bone."

"A-e, haho khang. Kea tseba hore ha ua etsa ka boomo hle khaitseli ea motho Leha ke silafetse ke nka ketsahalo ena e le bomalimabe bo lehlohonolo. Ka hoba ke tatile, ke kopa linomoro tsa hau tsa mohala ke tle ke u hloele ke utloe hore na ha ua robeha setho se seng sa 'mele."

"Ke hantle. Mohlolomong ha u ne u sa nkapa nkabe ke oele ka hare ho keribae eno ke le mong e be e kolumetse ka 'na, empa haho moo ho utloahalang ho opa": Pokanelo a araba.

"Motho o'a re ha a na bothata a thutsoe ke koloi e be oa shoa ha a fihla sepetlele. Kea kopa hle khaitseli eaka, hore feela ke tle ke utloe

32

na u tsamaile joang." Motebang o ne a bua a ntse a nyeka pounama, a bile a pasela ka ho roba leihlo. Kamor'a ho ngangisana nakoana e seng kae, Pokanelo ile a nolofala, a fela a fa Motebang nomoro ea hae ea mohala, ba nt'o arohana.

Motebang o ile a fela a etsetsa Pokanelo molaetsa mantsiboeeng oona ao. Ba ile ba qoqa hanyenyane eaba baa khaotsa. Ka letsatsi le hlahlamang ba ile ba tsoelapele eaba ho tloha mono eba molebe ho ea Swatsing. Ka mor'a nako e seng kae moqoqo oa bona e ne eka oa batho ba tsebaneng khaale, e ne e se e le oa batho ba ratanang leha hone hose ea kileng a re letho ho e mong ka taba tsa lerato.

Khoeli ea pele feela Motebang o ne a se a bua ka lenyalo khafetsa. Ka nako eno Pokanelo o ne a ntse a ena le mohlankana sekolong empa a se a tsoelipana ha a ea a mo lebile. Mabaka a mabeli a neng a etsa hore a mo qhome: la pele ke hore monate oo a neng a o utloa ha a na le Motebang, e ne e le o tsoellang. Bacha ba o bitsa *magic*! Taba ea bobeli e ne e le metsoalle ea hae e 'meli; 'Mamokhothu o ne a se a nyetsoe ha Mpaki eena a ne a fihle 'Mantaha o mong a kentse lesale monoaneng ho bontša hore mohlankana oa hae o ne a se a mo behelelitse. Pokanelo o ne a bona a salla morao ha metsoalle ea hae e tsoelapele. Moo a neng a lula teng le banana bao a neng a kena sehlopheng le bona le teng hone ho lutsoe ho itšoasoetsoa ka litaba tsa manyalo le bofetoa, athe eena o ne a li nkela hloohong.

Ka lekhetlo le leng e ne e re ha Motebang a bua ka litaba tseo tsa lenyalo, Pokanelo o ile a elelloa hore o tiisitse ebile o tatile. Motebang o ile a re ba shobele batla etsa tsohle ka morao. Leha mohopolo ona o potlakileng oa Motebang o ne o mo tsamaisa mafokoloi ka mpeng, ausi o ne a thabile. O ne a ipona le eena e se e le makoti e mocha 'me a qoqela basali ba bang ka taba tsa hae.

Pele a lumela litaba tseo tsa Motebang, Pokanelo o ile a inahana eaba o re: "feela ke lakatsa ho chata, hape batsoali ba'ka ba tla re eng ha ke se ke nyaloa ke sa qeta sekolong? Le lilemo tsa'ka ke hona li leng leshome le metso e robong!"

"Re tla feta *baby*, akere rea shobela kamorao re etsa mokete o moholo? Le sekolo u keke ua se tlohela. Ha re etse botoutu bo monate feela hle monna": hoa araba Motebang. Ba ile ba lumellana 'me ba beha letsatsi.

'Mapokanelo a hla a li hana ha a utloa litaba tseo nakong eo morali a reng oa mo utsoetsa. A raba-raba ka tlung a bua lintho li hana ho fela mosali oa batho. Ho thetha bohale ba 'm'ae, ke ha Pokanelo a mo kholisa hore o fetotse monahano.

La fihla letsatsi la hore ba nkoe ke 'mankhane baratani. Pokanelo o ne a lebe ha Motebang *litupulekeseng* hang ha lihlopha li tsoa motšeare. E ne e le hantle ka hora ea tinare. O fihlile morena a se a eme ka eena feela. Hang ha a fihla ba ne ba kene koloing, 'me ba kena tseleng ba hloa sehlaba sa Thuoathe. Koloi e purulelitse joalo hofihlela e tsoa sekontiring e kena tseleng ea kerabole. Thota e ne e namme 'me e khabile ka masimo a tletseng lekhaba le letle le letala la hlabula.

Pejana ho bona hone ho ena le sefate se seholo se neng se tloaelehile haholo litoropong le ha batho boholo ba ne ba sa se tsebe lebitso. Tikolohong eno ho ne ho le mohloa o matala tlaka! O tletseng lithung-thung tse ntle le meriana ea naha e ekhang 'mabolilana, tsikitlana le bo phate-ea-ngaka. Thokoana ho ne ho e na le mophulanyana oa metsi hape hona le linku tse ntseng li fula tlas'a sefate seo se seholo ha tse ling li buthile.

Ba fihla. Motebang a *paka* koloi tlas'a sefate seo eaba baa theoha. Hang-hang keha ho hlaha motho eo ho neng ho ipakahatsa hore ke molisana oa makhulo ao.

"Motho oa heso!": Motebang a cho joalo a atamela Molisana eo a bile a fihla a mo tšoara ka letsoho.

"Ntate!": ho araba molisana.

"Ke makhulo a hau a, kea bona a matala-tala?" Motebang a bua joalo a kentse letsoho le leng ka phokothong a ntse a lekola sebaka.

Molisana a rola mohlethe oa hae hloohong eaba ore: "ee oa hae, ke sona 'baka sa'ka sa boikhutso".

"Ke u fumane hantle, ke lumela o tla nthusa ka nthoana e nyenyane." Motebang a bua joalo a leba koloing, a bitsa Pokanelo, a bula koloi ka morao, eaba o re a bule mokotlana o motšo o neng o le ka moo. Ha a bula ngoanana a sala a maketse. Ho ne ho tšetsoe mose o mosoeu o molelele ba ho fihla lengoleng, le palesa e tšoeu ea hlohoong. Pokanelo o ile a thaba joalo ka lesea, a fofela Motebang a ba a fihla a imamarella ho eena a tšeha a sa emisi, likeleli li ntse li tšoloha mahlong a hae. Ha pelo e se e theohile, Motebang a mo kopa hore a apare mose oo o mocha, maotong teng a re a seke a roala lieta 'me le ena a rola tsa hae.

Motebang o ne a tenne borikhoe bo botšo bo bokhutsoanyane, hempe e tšoeu le sehara molala se setšo, eaba o kopa kharebe hore ba atamele sefateng. O ne a tšoere lipampiri ka letsohong la hae, eaba o re: "ke ngotse likano tsa rona mona, kea tseba ha ke li nepe hantle hobane le kerekeng ha ke ee, empa kea tšepa letsatsi lena le tlaba bohlokoa ho uena."

*

Leha Pokanelo a ne a lebelletse chobeliso e tloaelehileng, liketsahalo tsa tsatsing leo li ne li mo makatsa ka mokhoa o thabisang, 'me eaba lerato la hae ho Motebang le phahame hofeta pele. Motebang o ne a

35

mo bolelle hore batla robala hona moo e le ho keteka *hanimunu* ea bona hobane a ne a hloka mokhoa oa hore ba ee hole. Ba tsohile ka le hlahlamang mafube a se a hlahile, ba phutha mehasoana ea bona eaba ba kena tseleng ba leba moo Pokanelo a neng a lumela hore ke lapeng hab'o Motebang.

'Nete ke hore mono e ne e le ha e mong oa metsoalle ea Motebang. Motsoalle eo o ne a mo kopile hore a mo salle le ntlo ha a sa tsamaile ka mosebetsi. Ho feta mono Motebang o ile a kopa batsoalle ba hae ba bang hore ba itlhahise e le ba hab'o ba lelapa.

Ha ba fihla Motebang o ile a laela Pokanelo hore a kene kamoreng e neng e se e lokisitsoe. Ho se hokae batho ba qala ho kena batl'o bona ngoetsi, nku le eona ea hlajoa, eaba ho ngoloa lengolo le tsebisang ba hab'o Pokanelo hore na a batleloe hokae. Ntat'a Pokanelo o ne a halefe hoo a neng a khethe ho se ikamahanye. Eena le lelapa la hae ha baa ka ba ikhathatsa hohang.

*

Le pele beke ea pele ba nyalane e fela ho ne ho se ho'na le lintho tse 'maloa tse makatsang Pokanelo. Ea pele ke hore o ne a laetsoe hore a se bule lemati la kichini kamor'a hora ea borobeli bosiu.

Ea bobeli ke hore Motebang o ne a sa sebetse feela chelete eona o ne a na le e ngata ka tsela e belaetsang. Mantsiboea a mang le a mang ha hora ea borobeli e otla, potlolommente e tletseng chelete e ne e kena monyako ntle le qea-qeo.

*

Batsoali ba hae ha baaka ba ahlola Pokanelo ho fihleng hoa hae hae. Ba ne ba mo amohele ka lerato, hoo le eena a neng a phuthulohe eaba o ba joetsa tsohle. Hoba a ba bolelle mabitso a Motebang ka botlalo, ke ha ba ema ka sekhahla ba senyeha ka mahlong.

Ntat'ae o ne a laele bohle hore ba lule fatše hore a tsebe ho toloka pale ea Motebang: "Pele re aha mona ha Tšosane...", a thetha sekhohlela, a lulella qetellong ea setulo eaba oa bua. "Re ne re ahile motseng oa Morena Malopalle. Mehleng eo re ne re phela ka lekhulo le liphoofolo. Ho neng ho tumme haholo motseng oa rona e ne e le lipere. Lelapa le neng le'na le tse ngata le ne le nkeloa holimo hampe. Ha ele monna ea neng a ruile tse ngata ebile li le ntle, eena e ne e le monna har'a banna. Ka lebaka leno liqoaketsano li ne li le ngata lipakeng tsa metse, 'me ho ne ho hapelanoa tsona lipere tseo.

Ka le leng motse oa rona o ne o hlaseloe ka sehloho. Ha hoaka ha utsuoa feela empa ho ne ho senyoe lijalo masimong, batho ba bolaeana, le matlo a mangata a chesoa. E ne e le ka shoalane ha tsena li etsahala. Batho ba ne ba phase-phase ba tlala-tlala motse. Re ne re ena le ngoana a le mong oa moshanyana ea lilemo li tharo ka nako eno. Re ne re mathe ka eena re ntse re phomotsana le 'm'ao re sa bone le moo re eang."

Ha ntat'a Pokanelo a fihla karolong eno, 'Mapokanelo o ne a lle habohloko eaba Monna-moholo o mo silila lehetla ho mo theola moea. Pokanelo le eena o ne a lla habohloko ha a ellelloa hore e ne e le lehlatsipa la tlhekefetso matsohong a khaitseli ea hae.

Monna-moholo o ne a tsoele pele a re: "Har'a mpa ea bosiu re ne re fihle phulaneng e ngoe e bitsoang Phulana-licheche le ba bang. Leha re ne re sa bonane, ra ne re lumellane hore bohle re bokaneng 'moho re phomolele letsatsi la hosane.

Hoseng ha re tsoha, ba bang ba batho ba ne ba se ba ile, ho setse sehlotšoana se senyane. Har'a batho ba neng ba le sieo, e ne e le ngoana oa rona. Re 'matlile har'a batho ba teng empa ra mo hloka.

Mohlomong ka bongoana o ne a tsohe pele ho rona a tsamaea le batho ba tsamaeang eaba ha a hlokomele hore o re siile morao. Bothata e ne e le hore batho ba ne ba arohane likotoana ba tletse naha. Re mo batlile ra ba ra tela. Ke mona moo qetellong re ileng ra fallela mona eaba re hlohonolofatsoa ka lona."

"Pokanelo ngoanaka": ho bua 'Mapokanelo a qhela menyepetsi, "u fumane ngoan'eno. Ke masoabi hore e be ke ka tsela ena empa u mo thotse. Mohlomong tsohle tseo a li entseng e ne e le mohoo o tsoang botebong ba pelo ea hae hore ho be le ea mo utloang. Leha a u entse tsena tsohle, ke u kopa hore u fumane ka hare ho pelo ea hau hore u mo tšoarele ka le leng." Pokanelo ke ha a ema a leba monyako. "U leba kae joale? Pokanelo ema hle!": 'Mapokanelo a bua a leka ho mo thiba.

"Mo tlohele motsoetse, ha pelo e theohile o tla khutla. Esale re bolokile taba ena": Ntat'a Pokanelo o ne a bua a mo aka sefubeng sa hae.

Pokanelo o ile a bua ka lentsoe le fatše a re: "ha u palama bese, o e fumana e tletse batho ba mefuta eohle; barui le bafutsana. U khetha ho lula pela eo u mo ratang mohlomong hobane u bona a tšoanela boemo ba hau. Bohloko ke hore ha u tsebe mohlang u lutseng pel'a 'molai, kapa pel'a motho ea hantle. Ua tseba na hobaneng? Hobane liaparo, seemo, liketso le mantsoe a motho, ke tsona tse iponahatsang. Motebang; u ka tseba boemo ba leholimo naheng e 'ngoe e hole empa u le monna u keke ua tseba se kahar'a pelo ea mosali oa hau u lula le eena."

Motebang a ema fatše a mo atamela eaba o re: "athe u tseba lilotho ausi?". Pokanelo le eena a atamela eaba o re: "ha ke u lothe. Ke bua ka boemo ba bophelo boo ke ithutileng bona ka nako e khuts'oanyane, ka tsela e bohloko. Ke ne ke u rata. Mohlomong lerato la'ka le ne le 'tsoa ka hare ho mahlo 'me le phahamisoa ke seo u neng u se beha ka hare ho liatla tsa'ka. Ke tseba tsohle. Ke tseba tsohle ka uena, 'me nkeke ka hlola ke sheba bophelo ka tsela e tšoanang."

"Ke hantle ha u tseba tsohle": Motebang a bua a iphehla bohale. "Ho hlakile u tseba ho feta tekanyo. Le 'na ke tla u joetsa ntho e le 'ngoe. Ua bona lona banyana ba Basotho, le rata chelete hoo le sa tsebeng tlhalohanyo pakeng tsa eona le lerato. Motho oa teng ho hoholo ke ho iketsa ahlama-u-je. Le hore na chelete tseo li li tsoa kae ha le tsotella leha le ntse le utloa hore ho retloa batho. Pokanelo, na u kile oa nahana hore mohlomong hona le hlooho ea ngoananyana e mong e entseng hore ebe u kahar'a lichelete tse? Lea tšoana kaofela, haho le ea mongo oa lona a betere."

Pokanelo a bula molomo 'me Motebang a thola hang-hang: "Re bile re bangata? mohlomong hona le litaba tse tebileng le ho feta, tseo ke li fumaneng. Ha'eba ke eona tsela eo u phelisang basali ka eona ena, ke hore u ikopele liatla hobane 'khetlong lena tsena tsohle u li entse ho ngoan'eno."

Ha a cho joalo a seke a emela le ho utloa karabo ea Motebang eaba oa mo furalla o leba monyako. Pele a tsoa a ema eaba o re: "u sale hantle Thuso Mothabeng, 'M'e oaka, e leng 'M'e oa hau, o nkopile hore ke u tšoarela 'me ke tla etsa joalo.

Maseru City

M. V. Darko

2 Peter 3:10 --- *"But the day of the Lord will come as a thief in the night; in which the heavens shall pass away with a great noise, and the elements shall melt with fervent heat, and the earth also and the works that are therein shall be burned up."*

The city reeked of filth.

Angel could smell it in the buildings, as if the steel and concrete was rotting into a gray phantasmagoria of sin; greed. Entropy. The burg was small, and had prided itself as a peaceful place. Highbinder and pro-skirt alike scrambled for dirty coin, the type that could only be found in third-world countries. Dough that stank of failed coups, Home-Affairs bribes, and muddied election ballots. The ordinary Mosotho gink was more than willing to sweep his sin under the rug. A stinking, sun-kissed, *peaceful* tower of shit! But it was Angel's job to uncover that rug, and sock each demon that scrambled away from the intrusive light, one by one. It was an unfortunate job. But it had to be done. It was Angel's way of serving his Lord.

It was raining. No boiler, puppy or pro-skirt was seen on the street. The rain had forced them all inside, where they wallowed in the reek of their sins. Angel could *feel* them, like fucking wens growing on his skin. In a gin mill in Khubetsoana, two teenagers ground their private parts against each other, tasting sex for the first time. In an abandoned mall in Ha-Thetsane, a gonif fiddled with the lock of *Happy Dandy Emporium,* a suit store. In a big house in Moshoeshoe Π, a scrawny girl tricked her mother into R1.00 uncollected change from the spaza-shop. Angel could feel these sins, and they filled up his body like liquid. He regretted his reincarnation into Earth-Realm. He hadn't seen his son or husband for ten millennia now. *At least I'm dry,* he told himself, as the rain intensified its onslaught. Twenty minutes ago, he'd slurred an incantation that warded it off. His eyes pierced through the darkness with red lights, illuminating the path before him---an empty road, and even more empty buildings at the side of it. His eyes bathed the city in red.

Aharit Hayamim was coming, or as it was known in Earth-Realm, The End of Days. Ten millennia ago, just before his reincarnation, the JOYOUS TRIBUNAL had met at the Oval Court. Arguments had been made over a date. It had taken a thousand years, but the decision was finally made. Earth would end in the year [CENSORED]. The note was in a pocket underneath Angel's flogger, scrambled in God's messy handwriting. "Tell no one", God had said, and it was a mantra Angel had repeated over and over again, as if he was scared his thinker would 'conveniently' forget the instruction.

For now however, he would do his job, and the first assignment of the night was this:

Tiisetso Mohale lives in Tsenola.

Sex: Male

Race: Dinge (a.k.a "Black African")

Age: 36

Hair Colour: Black

Eye Colour: Brown

Build: Muscular

Occupation: Mechanic (mainly boilers a.k.a "automobiles")

41

In his village, his modest way of life earns him adoration. The villagers are poor, and he is poor with them. However, the true source of his fame is his looks. Women giggle uncontrollably in his presence. To the men, he is a secret god. It also helps that his tongue can spin gold (and lick vlodges).

Favorite hobby: lovemaking

Favorite colour: (he doesn't have one)

Best virtue: steadfastness

Worst vice: *hitting his wife.*

The rain was pouring harder when Angel arrived at Tiisetso's house. Lightning hammered against the dense clouds before being sucked back in. The neighborhood was dark; streetlights would only be installed in election season. Angel stepped into a puddle, but even that didn't make his boots wet. He could feel the soul of an emaciated dog slithering through the oppressive night, looking for shelter. It wouldn't find it. When the sun opened her vlodge, the dog would wake up dead, its body soaked full with leptospira and starvation. Angel knew this, just as he knew that in an obscure country far away, the Antichrist was being elected into office.

Tiisetso was poor man, though he liked to believe (and proclaim) otherwise. He lived in a three-roomed house. His front yard was filled with all sorts of useless shit, but to him, it might as well be king's gold. Bicycles twisted into obscure shapes. Used condom wrappers. The ground was so damp with oil that when the weeds moaned out, they grew black. But tonight, Angel would deliver Tiisetso's judgment.

He entered a dimly lit room. He found Tiisetso's kids entranced by the blinking television light (*WWE: SMACKDOWN!*). Angel knew all of them by name. He knew the sins that had been planted in their hearts already, even at that young age. He knew what kind of sinners they would grow up to become. Tiisetso and his wife, Senate, were in the house---Angel could feel their souls. He would deal with them. Shortly.

Just as the kids were getting worked into a panic, Angel moved his mitts in a strange pattern, casting a spell. He was altering their memories, freezing their life-blood in the process. Memory is like a song. It has high notes and low notes, tunes which murmur before exploding into tremulous sopranos. Angel's instruments were his fingers. He changed the shape of their memories---Lesotho---Sunshine---Laughter. Memories of a game called 'mantloane, laying brick over brick until it resembled furniture. A deepening of the voice where the father was being imitated. A high-pitched lilt where the mother was concerned. Childhood is a sickness filled with racing, screaming and sweating bodies. As he flipped through their memories, Angel thought of his own son, Ed. He finally saw himself in their conks---a man in a black flogger, with a small fedora to match. He had come inside their home without knocking. He wasn't human, that much was clear. Red lights shone nefariously from where his eyes should have been. As red light entered the room, Moshoeshoe, the youngest, opened his mouth, seconds away from a scream. Angel froze their life-blood. He erased himself from their memories, leaving the others intact.

Outside, the lightning crashed hard enough to cast pale light on the walls.

Angel entered another room.

He found Tiisetso and Senate in an act of love.

Hm, love Angel thought to himself, *even when the world is falling apart around them, human beings are still foolish (and horny) enough to*

43

seek its light. Senate's world was falling apart; it had been falling apart every day since Tiisetso put the ring on her finger. But Tiisetso was a man and men were good builders. Every night, he would rebuild their fortress of love only to smash it down again.

Even the make-up couldn't hide the googs around Senate's eyes, and youthful bruises on her neck.

They were on a tattered sofa, Tiisetso kissing her neck with wet sounds, building. She giggled softly, feeling her soul melt into his. Five cans of *Maluti* hooch lay opened at their gams. As horniness overwhelmed her, Senate kicked two down. The smell of hooch exploded into the room. Angel froze Senate's life-blood. It was time for Tiisetso's judgment to begin.

Tiisetso screamed.

The room was dark, so half his face was shrouded in red light from Angel's eyes. He stood up, shivering like a wet cat.

"I'm a praying man," he stammered.

His dick was out, and realizing this, he stuffed it back into his chinos. Angel was disgusted to the pits of his stomach. To think that this man...no... this *dissipated* man, had carried the seeds of his children in that vein-y, throbbing *dingus.* Angel had to admit---upon entering the house, he had thought them slightly beautiful. But they were born into a family of sinners. Pretty soon, they would descend into the same purgatory. Lesia: petty crime. Amohelang: prostitution. And Moshoeshoe (*ha! ha! ha!*) would put the Chicago Overcoat on someone else's shoulders, that old poetic sin: *murder.*

"We all pray," Angel said, sauntering towards Tiisetso, "But how many of us pray in earnest?"

Tiisetso grabbed the air, his usually chiseled mitts looking scrawny underneath the red light. Angel swallowed a laugh.

"No, you're w-wrong," Tiisetso said, "I could tell you of the m-many times I felt the presence of God in church. I know people who *murder* others!! They're the ones you should be focusing on!"

"You dirty skid-rogue," Angel said, "You would throw your fellow gink under the bus? If you were truly a church-man, then you would know what God says about loving thy neighbor. Of course, the Bible is just a fairy-tale. An infantilized history of Heaven, watered down to suit your substandard thinkers!"

"I'm a praying man," Tiisetso said, shivering in his entire body. "It's true."

"That doesn't matter!" Angel snapped. His voice was like acid, "I've come to seek vengeance on behalf of the God you've begged salvation from! And God doesn't accept prayers from *dogs!*"

"I'm not a dog!" he stuttered, indignant "I'm human! Like you!"

A slap broke through the air.

"I AM NOT HUMAN!" Angel roared, "If I were to show you my true form, you'd collapse into something more pathetic than you are now! Did you know that humans, like you, have gone insane just from looking at my naked body? They have begged for death! All of them, dogs! Dogs who begged for death, but death never came to save them! They salivated for her sweet song, and will keep salivating even when Hell freezes over from the Holy Light!"

Tiisetso slowly backed towards the window, his mitts held out before him. For a second, Angel thought his plan was to jump out, but then he remembered this was Lesotho, and Hollywood-suicides of the jump-out-the-window type didn't work, because every house was single-storied here. Tiisetso was trapped.

"I don't understand!" Tiisetso said, "How does God measure which sins are punishable and which are not? I dreamt about my mother last night and could tell she was speaking to me from heaven!"

Tiisetso was crying now. His mug was shiny with mucus and man-tears.

Pathetic.

"She told me I would go to heaven!" Tiisetso sobbed, "And it's not like I murdered anyone! I only hit them! I was only making sure they knew who was in charge!"

The time for chin was over. Angel's retribution began.

ANGEL'S RETRIBUTION: Don't try this at home

With superhuman speed, Angel was in front of Tiisetso, holding one of his mitts. Tiisetso lifted his other mitt and tried to sock Angel in the mug. It went right through, as if he'd grabbed a cloud of mist. Tiisetso groaned.

"You dirty, little dinge!" Angel spat. He broke Tiisetso's mitt with a loud crack. Tiisetso screamed until Angel could see his uvula.

Angel decided to let him go.

"Awwwwww, sheeeeeeet…" Tiisetso said, running around in circles. His mitt danced like a marionette.

46

"C'mon now," Angel said, "You're exaggerating. It's just a little sprain."

Within seconds, Angel was in front of Tiisetso again.

"No, no, no!" Tiisetso said, before Angel played him some chin-music. Tiisetso hit the ground with a dull THUMP! ---blood flashing in his kisser. Angel stood over his body. "Awwwww," Tiisetso groaned. Angel overturned him with his boot. Tiisetso's kisser hung limp. He made a weak attempt at covering his mug with his unbroken mitt. Angel lifted his boot, and jerked it full throttle into Tiisetso's mug. His schnozzle broke. Blood was released. Tiisetso wasn't handsome anymore.

"Does it taste good?" Angel said with a smile.

Tiisetso didn't answer (unfortunately).

"Wait till you see what I have in store for you," Angel said.

The magic began.

Angel held out his mitt before him. A high-pitched squeal filled the room, rattling the windows. Outside, thunder grumbled faintly. The air around Angel's outstretched mitt began to blur. If you had looked closer, you would have seen tiny, silver particles combining into a cluster. The squeal went louder. Tiisetso broke into a full, uninhibited cry, "Ngwaaaaaaaaaaa!"

An ax materialized in Angel's mitts. Sharp. Smooth.

"You like my new toy?"

Unfortunately, Tiisetso didn't answer again. Angel decided to do the talking for him, because blood was never silent. He wedged the ax into Tiisetso's noodle, his arms vibrating from the blow. A fountain of blood spurted forth, hitting the ceiling. The stream lasted for a while, until the blood turned a diseased black. When it lessened, Angel could see that brains had spilled out, tasting the Earth-Realm air at last. They *stunk* from depravity. Angel used all his strength to pull the ax out of the conk. He lifted. He brought it down again, breaking Tiisetso's jaw. Bone splintered and exploded. Angel lifted the ax again, and hit Tiisetso's pelvis. His pipestems separated from his upper body, leaving a sinuous trail of intestines. Angel hit Tiisetso again and again (he had died five minutes ago). The only sounds were the thuds of the ax against Tiisetso's squelching stiff. Angel couldn't stop. He lifted the ax again, thinking of Tiisetso's rebellious punches against Senate's face (*DID ANOTHER MAN COME IN MY HOUSE?!*). He lifted the ax again, thinking of Tiisetso's jealous mitts around Amohelang's neck (I'M YOUR FATHER! I WILL BRING ORDER IN THIS HOUSEHOLD!). Angel lifted the ax again and again. He hacked into Tiisetso's stiff until he was just a pile of meat. Blood was spattered on the walls, and blood ran around Angel's boots in a stream, and blood filled the room with its metallic, fleshy scent.

"I don't think I like you" were Angel's last words. He *reductofied* the ax and disappeared into the night.

When Angel left, Senate noticed that a change had come upon her husband. His eyes looked empty, as if he'd stared down a long, black tunnel only to absorb the blackness again.

"Baby, what's wrong?" Senate said, tugging at his sleeve.

She was quite horny, and Lord help her if he'd decided that her vlodge wouldn't do it for today.

Tiisetso stood up, tipping the remaining cans of *Maluti* beer over. It soaked in the carpet, as many tears had done before it.

"I can't stay here," he said, his voice parched, "I have to go."

"What?"

She stood up from the sofa.

"I have to go!" he said, "I can't tell you why, but I can't stay here anymore."

She knew that she was powerless to stop him. Men were good builders, and when they finished building in once place, they had to pack up their materials, and go and build somewhere else.

*

Something was rotting inside him; he could feel it eating his insides. Angel stood under the awning of *Ellerines* furniture shop, opposite the Cathedral of Our Lady Victories, a.k.a "glorified art gallery." He lifted a reefer to his parched lips, inhaled, and tried to empty his dome of every bad thought. The rain had stopped now, but the streets were still wet, glistening like they were made of diamond.

Someone was approaching.

The smell of damp piss struck Angel. It was Bushie; Maseru bum. Notorious for fingering broads on the sly for a couple of cents. Angel had an almost maddening urge to pull out his bean-shooter, and squirt metal into Bushie's brains right there and then. But he was harmless. Bushie drove a shopping trolley with all his worldly possessions inside, and had been wearing the same baggy clothes since Lekhanya, that shoe-shining, imperious idiot, had overthrown Leabua Jonathan in the coup-d'état.

"Greeting again Mr. Priest," Bushie said.

Angel didn't answer.

Bushie took a deep breath, "You remember my predicament I trust. I hate to keep bothering you, but I really need some of your magic. *Please.* I can't live on this earth no more."

He'd been asking Angel to bop him for five years now. He had tried committing suicide many times before, but had either failed (Exhibit A: Bushie's missing pinkie), or was too scared to carry the act through.

"Get out of my sight," Angel spat, lifting the reefer to his mouth again. He wasn't inebriated, but he was close.

"*Please,*" Bushie said, "I heard about how you helped the others. You're a priest after all. An angel. How will you do it? Will you fuck me in the ass or in my mouth? I can't live on this earth no more."

Yes, Angel had fucked the other hobos' asses, giving them T.D.D (The Drill of Death!!!),-but they were hopeless cases. Bushie didn't know it yet, but he had something inside that could lead him to an honourable life. Yes, Angel had seen it; a wife, a child, even a car! If there was any gift God had privileged these miserable, undeserving humans with, it was the idea of 'second chances.'

Angel was about to deliver the whole 'motivational talk' (unfortunately), when something stirred in the air (fortunately). Thunder grumbled. A breeze galloped across the empty, Maseru street. It was colder than any breeze Angel had ever felt, cutting through the bone marrow. Bushie, even with his substandard human thinker, knew that something was amiss. He could sense *evil.* He turned his trolley away with a screech, and scrambled into the darkness.

Angel didn't see him run (and trip) (*ow! ow! ow!*). His attention was turned to the shadows instead:

"Can't I smoke in peace anymore?" Angel said.

He heard the sound of high-heels *click-clacking* first.

"That is no way to greet an old friend," the voice said, "Of all the places you've hidden, I must say I'm impressed with Lesotho. For a moment there, it felt like you disappeared off the face of the earth. I'm curious; how did you find this place?"

"Doesn't matter," Angel said.

The demon appeared from the darkness. It had taken the visage of Palesa Leqebekoane, a 21-year old piece of skirt from Ha-Mabote. Palesa had died in a car accident on Mpilo Road two years ago. The demon living in Palesa's body was called Ardat Lile, and was infamous for sleeping with married, human men. By the time they discovered she was a demon, it was too late. Their semen was already dripping down the walls of her vlodge by then, and she would use it to give birth to Satan's children.

And the girl, Palesa, was an even sadder case. Her soul was locked in what the Spirit Dwellers of The West called an *impasse.* On the way to the Galactic Core, she had fallen in love with a recently-deceased Heath Ledger. Of course it was just an Incubus, and by the time its dick was inserted all the way up Palesa's spiritual vlodge, it was too late. The JOYOUS TRIBUNAL was in negotiations for her soul at the moment, citing her "an unwilling sacrifice at the hands of Satan's trickery."

"You found me," Angel grunted. "Now what?"

"Your etiquette has always been a prodigious event," she said, "How's Gabriel? And your son, Edward? What a beautiful boy he is. Do they know you're about to leave them for a talentless, Mosotho whore?"

"I have no interest in hearing your unsubstantiated theories, betrayer."

It was true. Angel hadn't done anything with the human broad. He'd only seen her singing in the gin mill, and thought of how soft her skin must feel. He'd imagined resting his ancient mitts beneath the flesh of her thighs. But she didn't know Angel, and Angel didn't know her either. That's the way it was supposed to be.

"If anyone is the true whore here," Angel said, "It's you."

That was true as well. Ardat/Palesa was screwing the leader of the free-world, George W. Bush. The worst part; he knew she was a demon.

She was about to speak, when Angel interjected, encouraged by the indignant look on her pan, "Even at my most immoral, I would be a *saint* compared to you. You disgust me! You truly disgust me! The universe cast you out the moment your nipples hardened for worldly pleasures. Now go and wag your saggy vlodge in someone else's mug!"

"My, my, my" she said, "If only God could hear you now. Is that the same tongue you deliver homilies with Mr. Priest? I won't let you waste your stale insults on me just yet, Angel. You know what I came for."

That was true as well.

"My answer is still no," he said, throwing the reefer into the darkness. There was a small, ember glow…slowly fading…before succumbing, like everything had done on this cursed earth, into the eternal night.

"But you haven't heard my proposition yet," she said, smiling.

He sighed.

"I'm listening, slut."

She walked closer.

"Your name," she said, "I know what it is."

Angel stopped breathing. He wished he hadn't thrown away his weed. He wasn't high enough, at least, not for this bullshit. He tried to smile, but his mug felt like tar. He knew what she was offering, and it was something that had haunted every spirit in Heaven for eternity upon eternity. When you reach Heaven, any memory of the past-self is erased. In Earth-Realm, men create religion in order to form a hypothesis about Heaven. A link. The conclusion of this hypothesis, the missing link, is 'death'. But the spirits in Heaven don't have any links with Earth. They don't know who they were in 'The Land of Before.' Many spirits were driven to insanity from this injustice, descending into an eternal state of being called 'berserk-mode' (of course the first spirit to be this way was a high-ranking angel called The Morning Star, known in Earth-Realm as Satan). But no such thing had happened to Angel. He never asked questions. He never rebelled. But then he'd seen the human broad. In a noisy gin-mill in Kingsway, her voice had cut through the heavy smell of hooch and staccato laughter from drunk, human ginks dizzy from their own self-importance, *"My funny valentine...sweet, comic valentine. You make me smile with my heart."*

"What do you want in return?"

He'd asked, even though he already knew the answer.

"The note" she said in a cold whisper.

Her eyes dropped to his flogger. He clutched it tighter to his body, under the irrational but very tangible fear that the note would burn its way through the cloth and land in her mitts. No doubt she would take it straight to Mr. Bush, and he would lick her vlodge in gratitude. A Bush for a bush. The world's politicians, scientists, and celebrities had booked seats on *The Mayflower,* 'The One-Trip-Apocalypse-Rocket-Ship' to Mars. The irony here? No one knew when Aharit Hayamim was coming, not even Angel himself. But the note underneath his flogger did.

But how harmless could *sin* be really? Angel had lived a fulfilling life, surrounded by his husband, Gabriel, and their son, Ed. They had lived together in eternity. What was there to eternity except...*more* eternity? More existing, yes, but not really living. Earth-Realm, on the other hand, was alive. Love. Death. Music. Debt. All these things, shrouded by the black cloak of the unknown, but nevertheless, alive.

"You can't run from your humanity anymore" Ardat/Palesa said, coming closer, "I can hear your heartbeat from here. It's soft... softer than a mouse's, but.....I can hear it."

Angel listened. A few seconds passed. Then suddenly, he could hear his own heartbeat as well.

The Earth is born in a cosmic womb. Creatures, odd and hairy, moan over the bereft plains. They are celebrating life. But they are also cursing it. The plants grow green. And thick. A playful mist catches in the sunlight, revealing weak rainbows. Volcanoes rumble, spilling their hot semen over the ancient ground. A dinosaur, the Tyrannosaurus Rex ...no, this is a bigger one. He is Prince of the Earth. He tears the flesh off a smaller dinosaur, as if it's made of cloth. The ground is groaning with dinosaur footsteps. But the Earth is hungry. She spits them out with a hiss. SEX---two Neanderthals tussle and combine on the hard ground. They don't have words to express their pleasure. The female creates one, and calls it language. It starts in low grunts. Consonants and vowels soon join the celebration. The Iron Age is coming. Adam and Eve's children migrate to new lands. They have sex in neon bars, and porno sets, and cavernous churches. WAR---dust is gathering on the horizon. It's the man called Napoleon Bonaparte, leading his army of corpses into the European metropolis. In Mississippi, Walter impregnates a fertile slave. That's when *he* (the baby) begins to understand the language of Earth-Realm. *He* (the man) grows up, and decides to kill every white man on earth. Robben Island---the metallic sound of freedom in cell 46664. The policeman's hat blocks out the sunlight, "You're free, Mr. Mandela." The whites flee to Australia or into the sea. CAPITALISM---Okies chase after the pale, Californian sunlight. It's the city where the angels are pert temptresses, actresses, porntresses, directresses, murderesses, junkieresses, prostitutresses, oh how I wanna be an actress! In China, smoke clogs the skies. The cancer has been planted in the Heart of The Earth. The Antichrist is coming, with his forehead emblazoned with the number '6', repeated three times. Repeated three times, over and over again, the number is repeated three times. Angel could feel it. He could feel everything all at once. And then, a lonely canary in a gin mill, singing in a blue dress, *"My funny valentine...sweet, comic valentine."* And the broad's name was Lesotho.

"What are you doing to me?" Angel said. He now realized that his knees had given in, and his mug, as sweaty as a cocaine-withdrawal, lay a few inches from the ground.

"You bitch," he grunted, "What did you do to me?"

"Make your decision," she said, her voice floating down to his ears, " I know your name. Do you take it?"

"Yes," Angel said, lifting the note up to Palesa's/Ardat's open mitt. In truth, he was begging for mercy.

"Your name," she said, "Is Tiisetso."

*

He paused.

"Baby, what's wrong?" Senate said, tugging at his sleeve.

They were in a sofa, about to make love, when Tiisetso's mind started to drift. His mouth was dry, as if all the saliva was suddenly drained from it. He stood up slowly, accidentally knocking over two cans of beer.

"I can't stay here," he said, his voice parched, "I have to go."

"What?" Senate said, standing up from the sofa.

"I have to go!" he said, "I can't tell you why, but I can't stay here anymore."

And this, dear reader, is the final lie that Tiisetso tells in this story. He knew exactly why he had to leave.

A link was formed. He knew Heaven. He knew Hell. He knew his place in the dimension-of-in-between, the place called Earth-Realm. Even though his name was Tiisetso, he knew he had a guardian angel that was part of him, and Tiisetso's other name was Angel. He had to leave, and he had to leave right this minute. He needed to find the girl called Lesotho.

In the sitting room, he found the kids watching wrestling. When they were alerted to his presence, Amohelang, his oldest, rushed to the remote control. She put the TV on mute. His youngest, Moshoeshoe, stood up:

"Ntate?"

He didn't answer. He'd hurt them so much already, both physically and mentally. His suffering, and theirs, would end today. He hugged each one of them, savoring the smell of cheap-soap on their skin. Tiisetso silently left the house.

Outside, it was raining harder. He had no umbrella on. The rain plastered his shirt to his skin, filling his ears with its drumming noise. But he felt warm. He walked deeper into the night, passing an overturned dog—stomach swollen with what he assumed was gas. That didn't matter. The only thing that mattered was walking. Tiisetso came from a family of violent men. Men whose body parts couldn't fit the puzzle of the world (*...the only thing that mattered was walking*). But he was different. Had had a Guardian Angel (*the only...thing...that mattered...was...walking*). He would find the girl called Lesotho (*the only...thing that mattered...*) and Lesotho would teach him how to love himself (*...was walking*). In a couple of days, the skies would burn red and the oceans would rage and never stop. But that was okay. He would begin a journey, an adventure. He would find the girl.

Tiisetso walked away from his past, enjoying the sensation of cool rain running down his face. The Earth could end as soon as tomorrow, but the future.......

The future was limitless.

"When you walk, your steps will not be impended; And if you run, you will not stumble"—**Proverbs 4:12**

KE TSHOMO KA MATHETHO!

The Ultimate Vengeance

Liyah Jan

My eyes burn and yearn to be opened, to revel in the breeze, to cool the sensation down. But the breeze is shut out as I try to swallow whole the river of tears that must never see the light of day.

This is the life I chose. Not that I had any other option. And now, it seems I have opened doors that should have remained shut. Now, I have to try all I can to close them. To let the flood flow inside while also doing my utmost to avoid being washed away in the stream of these tears. Easier said than done, but my life isn't over. Not yet anyway.

So I wake up and the heat of mid-November won't allow me to sleep. Too bad. Because the only serenity I find is when I'm asleep. My only saving grace. I cannot leave this bed. I close my eyes as one more time I wish for the cold embrace of death to claim me. But it won't. A long while I remain still and unsuccessfully try to convince myself that tomorrow will be different. I know better. If only. Come sunset and all my nightmares resume. Whatever did I do wrong to deserve this unending bitterness from life?

It's a Friday and he is coming home. I sigh as I finally garner the courage to get up and clean the mess I made last night.

"I want out! Seriously Motheo, I want out of this deal. I am done!"

"Are you sure about that?"

He doesn't even sound fazed at all.

"Yes I am."

At this point I sob uncontrollably into the phone in my hand.

"Yes I am. I need my life back. I have paid my dues and you know it."

He laughs arrogantly.

"Listen, you owe me. And until I decide that you don't, you owe me. Don't get it twisted."

I try my best to let a portion of absent serenity come over me.

"Please,"

Now I'm begging.

"Please don't do this."

"Don't do what? You are the one to blame for this predicament."

"I told you. I made a terrible mistake and I've paid for it. How much longer?"

"Until I say enough. So until then, don't dare be smart with me. I will destroy you."

The phone is still in pieces next to the door where it fell after I threw it against the wall last night. Fragments of the vodka bottle lay scattered on the thick expensive mat stained with red wine I spilled in a blind rage. I need an asprin. My head throbs with every heartbeat. Impossible how one can be a victim of such intense pain and still draw breath. And in all clarity, I know that taking my life will not be an escape from this. His rage will just simply be diverted to the ones I love and as selfish as I can be, I cannot allow them to carry the cross I put together.

There's a knock on the door and I know who it is already. I am late. She is not supposed to see this mess. I know she spies on me for him. She comes in and can not hide her questioning expression as she absorbs the mess in the room.

"Miss, is everything alright?"

"Not today, Thato. Don't pretend we both don't know who you're working for."

She seems rather shocked that I know. I carefully make my way around the sharp carnivorous glasses on the floor.

"When you're done, you may tell him that the phone is a mess. I need a new one."

I slam the door behind me and head to the kitchen. I pour a glass of ice-cold water and drink without a pause. Breakfast is already prepared by Thato and even though I loathe her, I am too famished to ignore the aromatic meal on the table.

While I eat, I think of what to wear tonight. It has to be to his liking. He's always very particular. I should check my cellphone to see what demands he has issued. But before then, I need a bath.

"Your bath is ready,"

Thato says, in a rather civil tone. I stand up and go to the bathroom without a word. Relaxing in the water with my hair held high in pins, I try to grant my thought processes a much-needed vacation, but I fail.

The iPhone starts ringing. I accept the call without uttering a word.

"You broke the landline."

"I see she wasted no time reporting to the master. It was an accident."

"Don't patronise me."

Silence.

"Why did you call?"

"To remind you that I will not be taking anything from you. That house is all yours. What you do with the deed is up to you. The car is yours. Whether you choose public transport, that's all on you. Either way, you will still do what I demand of you. With or without the material assistance, your choice."

"Are you done?"

He laughs. I want to choke him.

"Patience. Sadly, I won't be making it home tonight."

"What a surprise."

In a cheerful tone he says,

"Try to sound disappointed, will you?"

Silence.

"I do have a way to ease your loneliness as duty dictates."

My heart sinks. Not again.

"Be ready at 8 pm. Drive to The Hotel, the Presidential Suite. And wait. Oh, the colour is red. He loves red. Be sure to be blindfolded before he comes in."

The line goes dead. I rush out of the bathtub, head to the walk-in closet and shuffle through shelves till I find the small box and open it. Inside is a needle and a small bottle with a clear liquid. I fill the needle and inject the stinging liquid into a vein and suddenly feel dizzy. A high so good I smile in spite of my misery. Then darkness.

Upon waking up, I realise it is just 30 min before 8 pm. I wash my face and dress in the sleaziest red dress I can find. I rush to the garage and start the engine of my 2014 Audi TT. It roars out of Thetsane like a supercharged machine. I make it to The Hotel at exactly 8 pm and I rush to the bathroom to hurriedly apply my make up. I let the hair fall in heavy curls past my shoulders. The lips are blood red. Matte. Thick, perfectly shaped eyebrows and artificial lashes for a dramatic effect. I sit on the bed and wait. Moments pass by as I wonder what to expect. I hear footsteps. I quickly reach inside my red Gucci bag and pull out a scarf I tie around my closed eyes and wait.

The door opens and softly shuts. I can hear the soft sound of footsteps as he walks towards me. He takes my hand and stands me up. No word. Nothing. I smell the scent of a costly fragrance. Bvlgari. His breath is laced with heavy nicotine. A smoker. I want all my senses to die so I remember none of this. The last thing I need is yet another bitter memory to add to my overflowing library of nightmares. But I am alert. I should have smoked a joint. That way this would be bearable. I feel the sting of the tears in my eyes and do my best to hold them back for if I lose control, he will not be pleased in the least. He owns me. He controls me. I breathe when he says breathe. I blink when he says blink. I am his to do with as he pleases. And right now, as I have done 74 times before, I must submit to this stranger's demands as the tape rolls and my fate is sealed with every recorded frame.

After he is gone, I remove the blindfold and curl up under the shower in a bitter moment of yet another teary heartbroken session. Death, where art thou?

I slip back into the red dress and slowly drive back to a hell I call home. My gilded cage. As I park the car in the garage, I can hear the phone ringing inside. I run to pick it up.

"Just making sure you got home safely."

"Like you care."

"Of course I do. After all, *I am your husband*."

"Why don't you just divorce me? What good am I to you when you won't accept my apologies and instead pawn me off to your perverted friends like I'm a cheap whore?"

"I told you, I will divorce you when I'm satisfied that you have paid your debt in full. And as for you being a whore, you branded yourself as such when you cheated on me and got caught on tape."

"How many times do I have to tell you I'm sorry? It didn't mean anything."

"And yet you did it over and over again and even told him that you are just using me because I am wealthy."

"I said what he wanted to hear. Motheo please...it's not too late to work this out."

"What makes you think now I can ever be with you after you have been with so many other men and I have a stack of tapes to prove it?"

I begin to cry again.

"Don't waste those precious tears my love. They won't work. You'll just be dehydrated and I need you fresh and ready for another session tomorrow. Don't be as dead as you were tonight. Moan a bit next time."

I gasp in a mixture of horror and disbelief at the knowledge that he has watched the session already.

"Baby please, I'm sorry. I love you."

Even as I say it, my heart bleeds at the realisation that I mean it. I can't right my wrongs against him. He won't let me. And I miss the man he was before all this.

"Save it for your next client."

The line goes silent.

Yes, I have been an unfaithful wife to a man who was completely devoted to me. His only flaw was spending too much time away from home, making the money I spend lavishly with no limits. I know of the the compromising tapes that he uses to blackmail me into doing these shameful acts. Acts with repulsive men who pay him. The fees serve as payment for everything he ever bought for me. Every piece of jewelry. Every pair of shoes. Even the house and the car I am not allowed to return. He has taped every moment with every one of his clients. Failure to obey him will result in my being an overnight pornstar. I am so in too deep it seems both options I'm faced with are equally destructive.

I kick my heels off and make my way to the wine cellar and pick a random bottle. Back in the kitchen, I don't use a glass but instead drink straight from the bottle. Tipsy, I sit on the couch and drunkenly text Khahliso. The man who started all this trouble. He immediately calls.

"Are you sure you want me to come over?"

"Yes."

"But the last time you..."

"Forget what I said, my marriage can never be salvaged. Not anymore. I have to accept that and find a way to move on."

"I understand. I'm on my way."

Truth be told. I do not love Khahliso. What good is being faithful to a man who despises me? In less than an hour Khahliso is at my door and I let him in. I allow his kisses to numb my pain for a moment before I suddenly remind myself that I am a married woman.

"I'm sorry. I need time to sort myself out. I hope I won't be too late once my divorce is final."

"Not this time, Phapano. I am not leaving this house without you. Move in with me while you go through this divorce."

I look at him with teary ears and I feel so remorseful that I cannot do as he asks. As tempting as the offer is, I must decline. For both our sakes, for if I fail to do so, we will both regret it immensely.

"It's not that simple."

"I know. Complicated. That's what you always say. But how much longer?"

"Soon. Please be patient."

"What does he have on you?"

I choke on my words as I try to find a lie to take me out of this conversation. He doesn't know of the tapes or what shameful acts I have since done to buy my husband's silence. When he leaves, it is way past midnight and I still can't sleep a wink. I lock the door behind him and curl up in a ball on the couch, and yet, again I hope to die. And as I always do every morning, I regrettably wake up. Alive. Physically unscathed. Emotionally dead from feelings I cannot express. Carrying the dead weight of my sins on my shoulders. Sins committed against an unforgiving husband.

I suddenly feel sick and just as suddenly, a wave of nausea takes over me as I helplessly lay on my side and let it all out. Just then, Thato walks in and runs to my side.

"Miss!"

I let her give me a helping hand to stand up to go to the bathroom where she runs a bath for me and helps me in the bathtub. Carefully, she washes me and I'm too exhausted to push her away with my usual sass. I don't know why she is being kind to me. Maybe because she is paid extra for this. She gets me out of the bath and takes me to the master bedroom where she helps me in bed after forcing me to eat a bowl of oats and take an aspirin. Shortly after, I sleep only to be awakened by a ringing cellphone.

"I have had a long night. Please, let me sleep."

Then I hang up and he doesn't call back. Not until the next morning.

"You have to get up and go to a pharmaceutical and buy a pregnancy test. You are sleeping too much. And you cry too much."

How could he blame me? He has me working at odd hours of the night and I'm emotionally drained. And the prospect of taking that test is scarier than anything he's had me do before. I could be with child. By a man I do not know. I am always blindfolded during his despicable demands. Up until now I have succeeded to stay away from the public during the day in fear of being recognised by the faceless men who have had their way with me. Men I can never recognise. But now, I have my orders. I have to go. I take a shower and wear black yoga pants and an oversized hoodie, and drive to town. At the mall, I go to the toilets and take the test.

Positive.

I snap a picture of it and send it to him via Whatsapp as instructed.

"I'm coming home tonight,"

He says and hangs up.

As for me, I have no name to give my feelings. I drive back home in a blur and quickly fall asleep upon being reunited with my bed. I have no idea what to look forward to. But I am glad I am asleep until he waltzes into the room. I haven't seen him in 6 months. Not since the night he showed me the proof of my infidelity. And now, opening my eyes to find him sitting next to our bed staring at me, I don't know what to say. We remain silent. I don't know what he is feeling. He is wearing a poker-face and I am devout of any reaction.

"This is probably the last time we see each other."

Silence.

"If you have any final words to say, this is your chance."

I feel a stream of tears shamelessly make its way down my eye to my ear.

"I'm so sorry for everything I did to wrong you. To turn a good, devoted husband into who you have become now. I still hope that someday you will forgive me and give me a chance to be good to you like I should have been."

Silence.

"Right now it's impossible I know. You have caused me so much harm and blackmailed me and now there's a baby in our midst. I just want the hostility to end. The hatred. So if you won't forgive me, just go on and grant me a divorce so we can both start over. And I will let you go."

Silence.

"Not until you watch the tapes with me. That's the last demand."

I feel the shame creep up on me and engulf every inch of my being until there is nothing left.

"If that's what it takes, fine, Motheo, I will watch those tapes of countless men using me at your command. Just so this can be over."

"Yes, Phapano. That's what it will take for the hostility to be over,"

He sternly puts it. I have no option. So I watch him open his laptop and inset the memory stick as I steel my heart for the worst. It starts at the very beginning. The first night he had me drunk and sent his friend to use me. I was blindfolded. In all the acts I never saw their faces. 75 of them. Faceless. And now I'm about to know. I have no desire to know and have their faces imprinted on my brain.

"Please don't make me do this. Please Motheo."

"I told you. This is the only way it will be over. The only way. Unless you want the hostility to continue. Wipe those tears off and watch this."

I do as instructed. Heart heavy in my chest. He clicks play and I force my eyes to stay open and what I witness leaves me in absolute shock.

"It was you all along!"

I say in disbelief.

"Yes."

I'm still in shock.

"You let me believe it was others."

"I wanted you to suffer. But now I have to stop. I can't do that to our child. Tell me, do you still want that divorce?"

Hoja ka tseba seso

Nthabiseng Lucy Kolobe

Palesa o ne a holisitsoe ka makhethe ke nkhono le ntate moholo ba hae. Lelapa la'bo le ne le soko-sokola empa o ile a atleha ho qeta sekolong sa mathomo. Ka bomalimabe nkhono le ntate moholo ba ne ba so fihlele lilemo tsa ho fumana chelete ea maqheku, kahoo ba ne ba hloka mokhoa oa ho patalla hore Palesa a ntšetse lithuto tsa hae pele. Letsatsi le leng le le leng Palesa o ne a tsoha hoseng ebe o lula ka ntle o shebella bo 'mata'e ha ba feta ba ea sekolong. Ka le leng nkhono 'Malisebo o ile a hlokomela ka botlalo hore taba ea hose kene sekolo e ne e amme setloholo sa hae habohloko moeeng, hoo se neng se se se theohile 'meleng. Mosali-moholo o ile a fihlela tharollo ea hore a kope ntate-moholo Taelo hore ba rekise tšimo eo ba neng ba se ba setse ka eona. Kaha le matla a ho lema a ne a se a ba siile, monna-moholo o ile a lumellana le nkhono ntle le qeaqeo. Ka mor'a nako e se kae tšimo e ile ea fumana moreki, thabo ea eba e kholo lelapeng la ntate Taelo.

Selemo se secha ha se thoasa Palesa o ile a fumana sekolo 'me a sebetsa hantle haholo. Se hlahlamang seno ke ha a kopa nkhono le ntate-moholo 'ae ho tsoa motse a 'lo lula haufi le sekolo. Kaha ba ne ba mo tšepa, ba ile ba lumela. Selemong sa boraro a kena sekolo se phahameng, Palesa o ile a teana le mohlankana ea bitsoang Napo eo a neng a etsa selemo sa bone. Napo o ne a le litšobotsi li ntle hoo banana ba neng ba oela fatše ka mangole ha ba 'mona. Eno moshanyana o ne a tseba 'taba tsa hae hantle hobane Palesa h'a nka nako ho hapeha ka mor'a ho bolelloa kamoo a ratoang ka teng. Baratani bao ba bacha ba ne ba lumellane ho lula 'moho ka ntle ho tsebo ea batsoali ba bona. Lapeng hab'o Palesa ba ne ba ntse ba mo ngolla khafetsa ho utloa hore na bophelo bo ntse bo ea joang.

Hoseng ho hong, Napo o ile a kopa Palesa hore a mo nyale, 'me ausi a lumela kapele joalo kaha e ka o ne a lebelletse. Mohlankana o ne a botse ausi ka batsoali e le hore lipuisano tsa mahali li tsebe ho simolla. Palesa ke ha a se khitla sa motho ea otluoeng. O ile a bolella Napo hore eena ke khutsana-khulu kahoo mahali a hae a fuoe eena, etsoe batho ba mo holisitseng ba ne ba mo sotla hampe. Hobane Napo o ne a rata motho oa hae o ile a ananela kopo ea hae. Bo nkhono moo ba 'teng eaba taba tsa lenyalo ha ba li tsebisoe hohang. Lenyalo le ile la reroa le batho ba mengoa ka bongata, ha e se lelapa la ntate Taelo. Nkhono le ntate moholo ba utloile feela ka menyenyetsi hore morali o oa nyaloa, 'me taba eo e ne e ba tšoare hampe haholo. Monna-moholo ha a nahana tšimo eo a e rekisitseng ka mohopolo oa hore ha ngoanana a qetile sekolo batla phela bophelo bo monate, e ne eka a ka ipolaea. Ha e le motseng teng batho ba ne ba tšeha lelapa leo ba re le otluoe kaha le barali ba teng haesale ba ne ba nyamelle Khauteng. Palesa eena o ne a eja khobe ka lemao koana lenyalong le lecha a lebetse tuu ka batho ba mo holisitseng ka thata hotloha ha batsoali ba hae ba bolaoa ke lefu la AIDS. Ka 'tsatsi le leng ba hab'o bohali ba ne ba mo lulisi fatše ho utloa hore na ke hobaneng a ne a hloile batho ba mo holisitseng eaba karabo ea hae ea eba eo a neng a e fe mohlankana ha a ne batla ho mo ntšetsa mahali.

Ka mor'a likhoeli tse 'maloa ntate Taelo le nkhono 'Malisebo ba ne ba itete lifuba ba ea hab'o Palesa bohali ho ea utloa hantle hore na ke eng eo ba neng ba mo entse eona e le hore ba mpe ba kope tšoarelo! Ha ba fihla moo, morali o ile a ba sheba joalo-kaha eka o qala ho ba bona hona 'tsatsing leo. O ile a ba botsa hore na ba mo setse-setse morao ke eng kapa na ba batla ho mo bolaea joalokaha ba bolaile 'mae le ntata'e. Ntate Taelo o ile a ikutloa eka a ka mo fofela a mo thulana le

72

mabota ke bohale, empa o ne a sena matla a ho etsa joalo. Ba bohali ba ile ba leka ho kena lipakeng empa Palesa o ne a senyehile pelo ho se motho ea mo khonang. monna le eena o itse kare o mo pota ka nqena le ka nqane eaba ha ho nko ho tsoa lemina. Ntate Taelole le mosali oa hae ba ne ba tele, ba leba moo ba tsoang teng ba hloephetsa mamina ba sa qete.

Le ha ho le joalo, selemong se hlahlamang seno lintho li ile tsa fetoha lenyalong la Palesa. Monna o ne a se a fihla bosiu, a noa majoala, bohlola bona a bo pasa ka linaleli. Batsoali ba lekile ho kena lipakeng empa ba ne ba hamela letanteng. Ka lehlakoreng le leng Palesa le eena o ne a sitoa ho fa monna bana. O ne a ile a bolelloa hore o tla rehoa lebitso ha ngoana a le teng 'me seno se ile sa mo imela haholo moeeng. Hab'o lapeng maphelo a mosali-moholo le monna-moholo a ne a qepha ke lipelo tse bohloko. Ka le leng e ne e re ha nkhono 'Malisebo a tsoha hoseng a re o fa monna-moholo metsi a ho iphotla, o ne a fumane e se e le maobane, choba le letse phoka. Likhoeli tse tharo kamor'a mono eaba mosali-moholo le eena o ikela balimong. Ha e le lelapeng la Palesa teng litaba li ne li mpefale le hofeta ha a fumana hore monna o entse ngonana ka ntle ho lenyalo. Mong'a litaba ha a botsoa o ne a ikarabele ka hore eena a ke ke a lula le monna e mong ka tlung o batla mosali ea tla mo etsetsa bana.

Bosiung bo bong Napo o ne a fihle hae a tauoe hofeta matsatsi a mang, eare ha Palesa a re o mo hlaba lipotso eaba o mo fofela ka lieta le lifeisi. Palesa o ne a khakhathuoe hoo a ileng a tsoha a paka lithoto tsa hae hoseng ho latelang. Ha a fihla hab'o ke moo a neng a fumane ho se ho lula batho ba bacha ba rekiselitsoeng setša ke bo 'mangoan'ae ba Khauteng. Ke mona moo a neng a hopole hore o ile a nyaloa a sa tsebisa ntata'e moholo le nkhono'ae. O ne a hopole mohlang a ba tebelang ha ba ile ho eena hahab'o bohali a ba qosa ka hore ba bolaile batsoali ba hae. Tseo tsohle o ne a li hopola joaloka baesekopo ka kelellong ea hae.

73

VENEERED

Lerato Mensah-Aborampah

I remember shifting uneasily on that blue velvet couch that Monday afternoon. My eyes sailed nervously across the room as I took in everything I saw; every little detail in that room that would not have mattered had I not been as anxious as I was. I had to be nervous though - you would too if you were in my shoes then. I was going to have a meeting with a psychologist. I know that does not sound like a terribly nerve-wracking situation, psychologists are supposed to be the people with whom you can confide in. Well, under normal circumstances, perhaps, that is true, (not that I would know). I do not want to give you the idea that I am this psychologically struggling teenage guy who always goes for therapy sessions because I am not, well, at least I think I am not. My circumstance, believe me, was not normal.

That Monday turned out all wrong, which is probably an extreme understatement by any standards. The thing is, every typical school day morning, a student wakes up to prepare for school, with limited knowledge of the events of that day, except the memorised knowledge of the classes they will be attending. You wake up every Monday morning knowing that this day will definitely be different from the previous Monday in some way, in spite of the fact that almost every Monday your schedule is the same. If, for some reason, you decide to think of how drastically your day can change for the worst, there is probably a certain threshhold which you can imagine. I am certain that a worst case scenario a student like me can conjure about the day ahead, is, well, something along the lines of enduring a triple period of Math (which is one hundred and twenty minutes, by the way) by my teacher, Mrs Bosiu, who, in a very polite manner of speaking, is not what one would call charismatic. Or perhaps if you have attended a school like mine - where teachers are not reluctant to give you one to three lashes (at minimum, that is) on your hand or your behind when you are late for morning study or guilty of one thing or another - then the worst case scenario that your mind can fathom is getting one of those. This particular Monday of my eighteen- year old life is quite a story that altered my entire existence and I mean this very literally.

My buddies and I were lounging in the shade of the big tree near our dining hall during our lunch break at school that Monday. Rorisang came to us and called me aside. I stretched my arms to hug her but she stood still. I could hear my friends giggling and I ignored them. I was happy to see her until I saw her distraught eyes. Holding her arm, I led her away from my friends who were beginning to make those silly whistles that boys make. When we were at reasonable distance from them, I cleared my throat and asked her what was wrong. I was slightly anxious because it was evident that she was not herself. The perky and radiant Rorisang that I knew was not the girl who stood before me. Something was amiss.

"Babe, what's up?" I asked soothingly. She looked away, avoiding my anxious gaze. I tried to reach for her hands like I always did when we talked, but she kept them to herself. I noticed how she fidgeted nervously with her fingers and tapped her foot time and again. Then I knew that I really had to be worried.

"I will wait for you at the gate," she paused and sighed heavily, "Reff, we need to talk." With that, she turned and walked quickly towards the classroom block. Most boys agree that when a girl says, 'we need to talk,' there is trouble. We dread this three word statement. Regardless of its abruptness, it is usually a strong signal of imminent disaster. As you can imagine, the suspense was killing me. That afternoon, I barely concentrated in class. Throughout the eighty minutes of Mr. Sefali 's chemistry lesson, which was usually my favourite class, my mind wandered off into unending tunnels of unanswered questions.

Was she breaking up with me? She would never do that though, I remember thinking. I had to be the only guy for her in school. Besides, 'I' was the guy so 'I' had to do the dumping. Yet, if she did, then my reputation would be tarnished. You probably think these were all petty thoughts. You have to understand that I was dating a girl who according to most people was the 'hottest' in high school. I did not want to be known as the guy who got dumped by Rorisang Sebeko, the girl whom most high school boys wished to call their own. There was no way I would let that happen - she was mine. My ego, my image, my social status at school were at stake.

The 15:20 alarm shook me out of my thoughts and I quickly rushed to the school gate. Rorisang was already there, leaning against a low brick wall, her eyes redder than before. I held her arm and we walked to a spot that was more private, under a big metal board that had, written on it, the name of our school. Some of our schoolmates cast glances at us but I did not care. People always cast glances at Rorisang and I when we were together.

"Roxy, come on now, talk to me," I began, feeling a lump of manly fear build up in my throat. She sighed heavily. Her big, brown eyes were slightly swollen. She had been crying.

"Reff, I...I...," her lips were shaking and tears began to flow down her prominent cheeks. Momentarily, she closed her eyes as if drawing a hefty amount of courage to say whatever it was she needed to say. Then finally, in low-pitched voice she said,

"Reff, I haven't had my period in two months now." She kept silent after that, letting me figure out the meaning of her words. I got what she was saying but I did not want to hear it. I did not know what to say so I decided to play silly and funny.

"So, why are you telling me this?" I managed to force a little laughter, "Roxy, I think it's high time we set a few things straight - babe, we can survive this relationship even if we don't share those known but not-spoken-of girl things come on now." I smiled. Rorisang disregarded my failed attempt at humour. She ran her hand through her neatly-plaited corn-rows, an obvious act of frustration.

"Reff," she bit her lip, "Reff, dude, I am pregnant!"

My mind failed to contemplate the enormity of the sentence, 'I am pregnant.' My first solid thought at that moment was that she was joking. She was playing some sick prank on me. Yet, if she were, then she had a very funny way of doing it for she looked dead serious. This 'solid' thought dissipated almost as soon I had thought of it. We had been seeing each other for quite some time, Rorisang and I, and if there was anything I certainly knew about her, it was that she had to be one of the most hopeless liars I knew. I looked at her closely and I realized that her relentless sobs were not a joke. She reached for my hand, held it and squeezed it and looked straight into my eyes as if searching for an answer, any reaction or response from me. I gave her nothing. My face must have turned pale instantly. She raised her lips to say something then decided against it. Rorisang allowed her hand to slip away from my frozen palm. She cast one last, helpless glance at me before disappearing into the crowd of students going out of the gate.

*

I clearly remember that afternoon and not having the slightest idea what the feelings that were brewing in me were called. I walked out of the school gate in utter confusion. I did not want to meet any of my friends so I headed home, taking the road that leads towards a neighbourhood at the west end of town. I was overwhelmed by complex feelings; each of them screaming silently in me, demanding to be heard. I knew of a lot of guys who had abandoned girls they impregnated, but I had never entertained the idea until that moment. The thought did eventually cross my mind. I considered the possibility that Rorisang was just mistaken and was not pregnant at all. I even considered the possibility that even if she were pregnant, I was not necessarily the responsible party. These feelings flooded simultaneously into mind, giving me no chance to actually sort them out and devise a strategy.

I was angry at myself. One reckless mistake was about to conceive a messy future for the both of us. Of course, I thought my future already did not promise much because my grades as a Form E student were unlikely going to get me into college. The irony of the situation seemed to mock me viciously; a high school boy like me, who was barely able to create a solid plan for his future had successfully created a human being. I knew this human being was merely an embryo then, but the point is, the formation of an intricate embryo should have been beyond my capability.

Another feeling shouted the loudest. A feeling that I tried to brush off or even suppress. Guilt. I clearly remembered that night at Thabo's party, in the noisy and crowded house. Even when she had showed a slight hesitation towards the idea of us sleeping together, I had managed to persuade her.

"If what we have is real, then this merely attests to our affection. What's the worst that could happen? " I had said to her. This guilt lingered, creating an intense turmoil within me. Yet, that is when I began to cowardly wonder why, like other boys, I too could not just leave Rorisang to deal with the situation on her own. I mean, for all I knew, the real father was probably not me. Me not being the father was a reassuring prospect, however one that did not succeed in allaying my guilt. I knew Rorisang and deep down I knew that the guy responsible for the human being gradually taking form inside her was me.

*

As I walked past State Library, I realized that the entire time I had been walking, I had been totally oblivious of my surroundings. You could swear I was in some state of trance. Ten minutes later, I was walking by Shoprite. This is the part of my story that, even today, I don't understand. My eyes happened to land on this big metallic board attached to the side of a building. On it was written, in bold letters;

FREE MINDS pty. Ltd, Psychologist Sessions, 08:30 - 17:00

It was a spontaneous decision. Of course, the idea of seeing a psychologist was never in my wildest thoughts. Perhaps I felt I needed to talk to someone- anyone who didn't know me. Rorisang always told me that I was different from other boys because I could talk about my feelings. Most people think that reticence is a 'manly' character. I happen to not fit into this notion, and yet I am a man - a young man, who sadly, has made some load of careless mistakes.

The truth is, the chaotic feelings in me were gnawing at my conscience. I had to talk to someone. I guess I figured that it was better and safer if that someone did not know me. That way, they would judge me less harshly. I remember taking the elevator to the fourth floor, then speaking to this cheerful woman at the reception. I recall the surprised expression that immediately took over her face when I talked to her. Ultimately, she had smiled comfortingly at me, telling me not to worry because the psychologist was not too busy that afternoon. I stood by her table while she made a call. I do not clearly remember what I had said to her when I arrived or what she had said to the psychologist on the other end of the line. My mind seems, however, to have taken note of phrases she said like, 'quite a young man,' 'looks pretty shaken up,' and, "no appointment.'

After her talk on the phone, she looked up at me with a big smile. "Forget the payments, young man," she said light heartedly, "The psychologist says you can go in." Her distinctly sympathetic eyes directed me to the grey-framed door of the psychologist.

So that is how I found myself in a psychologist's office. However, had I known the outcome of my spontaneous arrangement, I assure you, I would have never set my foot in that building.

*

I remember shifting uneasily on the blue, velvet couch that Monday afternoon. My eyes wandered around the room curiously. The bookshelf that stood against the wall, opposite to me was packed with books about nothing but Psychology. My eyes scanned the spines of the books and as expected, there were titles like, *Tap into the Mind* and *Liberate Your Mentality*, I noticed that the bookshelf was peeling off at its corners. Underneath the shiny, vanished plaster, its rough, unfinished surface was exposed, and for some reason, this made me realize that sooner or later, the truth always has a way of emerging. I had no plan whatsoever concerning Roxy's pregnancy. I did not know what I had to do, but rest assured, our secret would be exposed.

I observed the colour combinations used in the room. A pastel colour-

lilac distributed evenly on the cushions and window rails. A beige carpet with geometric motifs spread out through the entire room, seemingly giving the room a sense of vastness. I admit, the daunting situation did make me observant – too observant.

The door behind the psychologist's big wooden table creaked open. I figured it probably led to his kitchenette because he came out holding large mug of coffee. I literally jumped from the couch as he entered. He slowly approached me.

"Young man," he said, in a deep and hoarse voice, stretching out his frighteningly outsized hand to shake mine. I swallowed hard. It was evident that he was the kind of man who could instantly crush anyone or anything in his way. Cautiously, I stretched out my hand to his, grimacing as I felt the strong grasp of his shake.

He sat on an armchair across a glass table from me. The chair creaked under his weight as he shifted in an attempt to settle. He was, indeed, a heavily built man, probably in his late forties. I could not help but eye his muscular arms which had almost stretched his cardigan taut. His freaky robustness honestly scared me. How his patients were able to feel at ease when his presence seemed to harbour this intense authority, was a mystery to me.

It was about that time when I began to feel utterly stupid. What in the world was I doing there? I mean, how was I even going to explain that I had no appointment, even worse, money? Was I really going to tell a stranger that I had made my girlfriend pregnant? I knew very well that both our parents were likely going to kill us. Rorisang had told me a lot about her strict father. He apparently, tolerated no nonsense in his house. I wondered what she was going through at home, and if she had told her parents or was even intending to. I was in some mess.

"Ok son," he began, staring curiously at me behind his black framed spectacles. He seemed to be scrutinising everything about me. I felt exposed. He probably had some techniques for assessing people even before they started talking, he was a psychologist after all, right? I looked away, afraid that he would read my messy life on my face. "What's up?" he asked casually, leaning back on his chair. He smiled warmly and signalled, with his big hand, that I should start talking. I rubbed the back of my head and began,

"Eh...sir...I am Refiloe and I don't exactly have a reasonable reason why I am here, plus I'm flat broke so I don't think I'll be able to..."

"Refiloe, son, take it easy," he suddenly interrupted me in this strong voice which, in spite of the authority it possessed, was not at all frightening and imposing like his muscular physique. "This is one of the strangest things that has ever happened to me in my fifteen years in this job," he chuckled, his laughter softer than his voice. "A teenage boy with no appointment or money bringing himself to a shrink?!" He shook his head in disbelief. Smiling and clearly amused, he continued, "Son, this is crazy, you realize that?" I hung my head as the silliness of the whole situation made me feel more stupid by the second.

"But you know what - I've got the time. Just talk, son."

The way he kept calling me 'son' was rather irritating, I must say. It made me get this feeling that he thought I was pathetic, which was probably the case, but it was irritating nevertheless. In a strange kind of way, however, I was beginning to feel a bit comfortable in his casual, amiable presence.

I scratched the back of my head. I had to start talking. *What in the world am I doing?* I remember thinking to myself. I sighed deeply.

"Thank you Sir... here is the thing," I tried to fix my eyes to the floor as much as possible. "Well...eh...you see my girl... I mean my girlfriend...she is...she told me she is pregnant." I heard the creaking of the armchair again as he shifted. He took a sip of his coffee and appeared to listen more intently.

"I am as good as dead because my parents are bound to end my life when they find out and her dad is probably going to kill me - just to make sure I'm deader than dead I guess." I remained silent, waiting for him to speak about my recklessness and all that. I began to feel tiny surges of anger. We had used 'protection' of course, so what had happened? Rorisang was most likely going to leave school. She would come back only for the Form 5 final examinations in November unless we found another way. I began to wonder whether her well-planned future was on the verge of dissipation and whether she would be able to handle the stares and whispers everywhere she went. There was absolutely no way in which people would not find out. It was inevitable. I cast a glance at the psychologist whose eyes had been boring into my forehead. "I guess I am worried about her, you know, I am. I mean if she is pregnant...*eish*, I have never been in a situation like this, you see." As I said all this, I realised that I was actually more frustrated than I was aware of.

The psychologist leaned closer, as if I had started quite an intriguing topic. I saw a little smile form subtly on his lips. I did not blame him though, I bet it was not every day that boys showed up out of nowhere talking about pregnant girlfriends. He stroked his well-trimmed moustache, then spoke in an impressed tone,

"This is something else. Son, I have never heard of a boy so concerned about a pregnant girlfriend and that tells me a lot about you young man." He smiled at me knowingly. I was slightly suspicious about his last statement. What could he possibly conclude about me? Either he really thought I was a responsible boy who was willing to own up to his mistakes or like many other boys, I was only feigning concern when in actual fact I was trying to save my bacon. To be honest, I did not even know which boy I was.

He put his large mug of coffee on the glass table and gave me a concerned look.

"Refiloe, I'm not going to be of much help to you. My boy, you are what? Seventeen, eighteen? Yuh? What are you going to do? It is, after all, your life," he stared at me with this confidence in his eyes - confidence in me, in my decision. There was a moment of silence. This silence meant he was waiting for an answer to his question, which, of course I thought was rhetorical. What was I going to do? What kind of question was that? I did not know what I was going to do! I was no less confused than any madman in the streets of Maseru. I began to press my knuckles. I had no answer.

"Refiloe, tell me. Do you love this girl?"

I actually felt sweat prickle from my armpits and I finally blurted out,

"I do. Yes, I guess...I mean I think I do. Well, love...I just..." I was stammering like a six year old. So I was pathetic, I know. The thing is, the word 'love' which was obviously not a new word, did startle me a bit. For it was the first time I became fully aware of the commitment that hung around that word. Love, I concluded, was deeper than I had thought. What did I really mean when I told Rorisang I loved her? What did she mean when she told me she loved me? She was beautiful and attractive. I loved being with her and I guess I did love her, but I remember wondering what the word even meant. He laughed slowly.

"Boys," he said with disappointment, "you 'love' when it's convenient for you, don't you?" He took his mug and stared into it for some seconds then finally looked at me. I hung my head. I could sense the tinge of disapproval in his voice. "So tell me, son, tell me an obvious thing, if you are not the pregnant one, why are you so bothered?"

I stared at him like he was crazy. What kind of question was that?

"Because Sir," I replied, my voice betraying the absurdity that I felt his question harboured, "I am the one who got her pregnant, of course."

"Khotso – that's my name," he said. I realized that I had not even known his name till then. I sat on the edge of the couch, resting my elbows on my knees. He smiled a bit. "A silly question, you reckon? Refiloe, son, are you bothered so much because you know the implications of this pregnancy in this girl's life and yours too, or is this frustration you feel merely because you would rather have her deal with all this on her own?"

I looked at his eyes which gazed intently at me behind his thick-lensed glasses. He was making me think thoroughly about the reasons behind what I was feeling. I began to feel like he was making me feel worse than I did already.

"Ntate Khotso, with all due respect Sir, you seem to be saying that I do not have Roxy's best interest in mind? Is that what you are saying sir?" I rubbed the back of my head and he just remained silent.

"Ntate Khotso," I continued, "I know that she was a bit hesitant towards...you know," I was ashamed. It was an awkward situation. I cupped my hand to my lips and mumbled, "I guess I do feel guilty." I wanted to continue, but the urge to defend myself surfaced. This whole thing had two parties involved; Rorisang and I. She could have refused but she did not. Why did I have to feel like to the villain and her, the saint?

I straightened my shoulders in defiance, "But this isn't just my fault! She could have said no if she didn't want to, right?"

He looked straight into my eyes, "You are right. She could have said no, in fact, as an adult, I say your Roxy should have said no. She didn't. It's her fault too, without a doubt!" It felt good to hear him say that. He stroked his moustache, looking at me as if he were thinking very deeply about something. He finally said, "I want to know though," he grinned, "you didn't use that lamest line in the book, did you?"

I stared back, dumbfounded. "I am not following, Sir."

"Tell me, you didn't tell her that sex would prove she 'loved' you, did you?"

Silence.

"Refiloe, you realise that you call it 'love' when it suits you. Ironic, don't you think?" He sat on the edge of his seat. Some of his words bounced from one wall of my heart to the other, triggering in me endless questions. Did I really love her or did I merely tell her I did because I wanted what I wanted? She also would not have done it unless she wanted to too, I suppose. I had still told her I loved her way before we slept together anyway. Would I have even doubted this love had she not fallen pregnant? Why was the whole concept of love being challenged when there was pregnancy in the picture?

"Well, maybe I do love her, okay?" I said, unaware of how loudly, "maybe I do, I don't know!"

He took off his spectacles and rubbed them against his grey cardigan, then put them back on. He crossed his legs and said, "Son, I have been your age and I've seen enough in my years of life to know how a male's mind works. I've counselled couples who tell me they fell in love since their time in high school. So I do not deny that love can exist between girls and boys your age."

He paused momentarily and then spoke more slowly as if he had carefully thought through every word he wanted to say, "Son, I know this; love is one of the most powerful and profound forces this world has ever known. It is immovable. It is unshakable and it is definitely an epitome of the infinite. But I want you to understand this, love is a choice. Love, my boy, chooses to stick with a person amidst the craziest situations. And son, you are in some crazy situation. You and this girl."

He put his large coffee mug on the glass table. "If you love a girl," he continued, "you love her enough to respect her and stick with her even in the messiest situations, especially when the mess is caused by the both of you." He rose from his chair. I stood up too.

"Ntate Khotso, you think I do not love her?" I asked.

"All I am saying is, your love for this Roxy will be confirmed or disproved by whatever decision you will take."

I did not realize it at first, but he was slowly putting some emotions within me ablaze; I felt guilty already and I felt like he was worsening the guilt. He was like this emotionless prosecutor who could make an innocent person on the stand to ultimately think they are guilty.

He walked to his black, leather chair behind a large wooden table, with office things neatly arranged on it. He flipped through some files on his table as if I was not even there before him.

"Ntate Khotso, if you were in my shoes right now, wouldn't you want to find the easiest way out of this mess?"

He raised his head from the files and looked at me, his eyes pierced mine. He spoke in a firm voice, "You are in form 5, I suppose?" I nodded. "This girl too?" I nodded again. "I am certain you are fully aware of the implications of this pregnancy. Refiloe, son, you are responsible. You know that your girlfriend is carrying your child. I reckon you are torn between abandoning this girl to solely deal with this mess that both of you got into, and doing what you know is right. Son, you need to get your game together and do the right thing."

He made a deliberate effort to articulate the words, 'the right thing' so I could not miss them. I remember being terribly annoyed by Ntate Khotso. Emotions overpowered discretion. Unaware of how much anger was evident in my voice, I said,

"What do you mean by 'the right thing? Really, Ntate Khotso, what is this 'right thing' you speak of? Have you ever even been a situation like this one or are you merely telling me what a psychologist would tell me?" My mind was spinning fast, unable to process the words that gushed out of my lips. "I feel like all this weight is placed onto my shoulders! If Rorisang Sebeko knows what's best for her - for us, she had better get rid of it!"

The transformation that took place on his face was drastic and sudden. I swear I remember seeing his dark face turn red. In a fleeting moment, before I could even make sense out of everything, he had grabbed me by my school shirt. I was so close to his face that I could smell his breath that reeked of strong, black coffee. I could see the veins protruding around his widened eyes. Almost immediately, from the corner of my left eye, I caught a glimpse of shiny, silver metal nailed onto his tabletop. It was boldly and I am certain, clearly inscribed for me:

MR. KHOTSO SEBEKO- PSYCHOLOGIST

Sebeko? I swallowed hard. The surname kept bouncing in my cerebrum, which, at that moment, had managed to deduce a plausible reason to why my feet were dangling a few centimetres form the carpeted floor. My mind conjured certain truths that were rather frightening, amongst which one truth was clear - I was as good as dead.

Samaritan

Khosi E. Rajeke

"Kind sir, got some Adams by any chance? Grannies, more specifically...please."

Just today, the 1st of June, the prestigious Winslow restaurant was teeming with people. Postgraduate students had cluttered their tables with old notepads, porcelain ashtrays and a mosaic of scholarly journals. A pervasive scent imbued with a faint smell of coffee and cigarette smoke hovered above them. Loud voices, emphatic conversations and the occasional cackle had evidently become their charge. A freshly washed Granny Smith sat conspicuously at the edge of the table. Members of faculty were dressed in pristine academic regalia. The purists had on other paraphernalia of academic prestige, as per tradition, such as embellished brooches and medallions to reflect their status as academic elites.

Members of the public made up the majority of the multitude. The lowest tier, the middle class and the highest echelon of society had representation. Waiters went around offering the guests refreshments and manoeuvred to and fro between the kitchen and the vastness of the dining room. The atmosphere was relaxed. I used the light background music to help me think about how many drops of water had been imbibed by Hisenryzer's "Analytic Hierarchy Processes in Identity Formation" article I had put my apple on. More importantly, I pondered the boldness it must have required for one person to challenge the conventions of an entire people.

A man walked onto the stage and all attention was shifted towards him as he approached the lectern,

Ladies and gentlemen, my name is Johannes Hisenryzer. I am the director of the Centre for Anthropology and Policy Studies. It is my singular honour and privilege to be with you on this momentous day. The Winslow, as you know, ladies and gentlemen, has a longstanding reputation for hosting public debates and critical dialogue such as our agenda this afternoon.

Applause swept across the audience and he continued with renewed fervour,

Our invited speaker is neither a stranger to this institution nor to the public. Indeed, who can forget his most recent enterprise? But, ladies and gentlemen, this is hardly an indictment of his actions.

Professor Hisenryzer is perhaps the youngest among his colleagues. He is a dark-skinned, fastidious man with an overbearing demeanour, as close to godliness as cleanliness can get him. He is generally hard to read, but anyone who has studied his work can attest to his genius.

"Dear colleagues, distinguished guests, without any further ado, it is with great pleasure that I introduce our speaker, Mr. Eric Wabachei!"

A steady round of applause filled the room. As the guest left his table and began to make his way to the stage, professor Hisenryzer went on enthusiastically, the smile on his face eerily out of character, "Mr. Wabachei is one of our most eminent alumni and we are thoroughly delighted to have him here."

He stepped away from the lectern and the men took a seat on two exquisite chesterfield flat wing chairs accompanying a matching Noguchi table at centre stage. On cue, the lectern was lifted off the stage. Silence fell upon the audience and anticipation built up. Mr. Wabachei appeared to be no older than the professor and a resemblance showed in their physique.

"On behalf of the Ishacru Institute, I would like to welcome you, Mr. Wabachei. I cannot adequately express how excited we are that you are in our midst."

"The pleasure is all mine, professor. As you have rightly said, I pursued a significant portion of my studies here, and the Winslow has always been one of my favourite places on campus."

"Due to the current paradigm shifts in our society which, some would argue, were given impetus by your speech at the city hall, the Centre for Anthropology and Policy Studies considered it in the public interest to invite you for a brief dialogue."

"I am excited to be here."

At this juncture, the audience paid close attention to the exchange. My peers had turned note-taking into a display of industry and my apple sat close to the table's edge, half-bitten.

"Some people are curious about who you are, Mr Wabachei. Perhaps you could give a background of your upbringing and we can take it from there. A short Q&A should conclude our session."

"But of course. We can start with my name, 'Eric Ofeng Wabachei.' I do not know how many 'Eric Wabacheis' I have met over the years."

He tilted his torso a little to face the anxious crowd and something in his countenance changed almost immediately.

> "Philip, Ian and I called ourselves the 'Elastic Band'
> because of how we would stretch ourselves in the

library and then shrink to fit in the world again. We could make a fort out of any reading space. Ian was a seeker of God and pathfinder while Philip was friend sent at the right time. They and I met during the laborious year my family spent on the road seeking refuge. We eventually settled in the south. It turned out that we shared kinship with a clan in the region and they made a case before their chief for us to be granted a community of the land.

"I was about eight when they took us in. The kids there used to call me 'moholo' meaning that I had an old man's soul and it used to baffle me. My friends and I were somewhat an oddity. Philip was a great explainer, Ian was full of love and rebuke, and I was the glue that held the group together. Nonetheless, some of my peers, friends, would claim to know me without ever having had shed tears from peeling this onion, but I did not mind. Ian and Philip are the best friends I have ever had. We did not move here until I was seventeen, right after I finished high school. In anguish, I had to abandon my newly found belonging and leave my grandmother's love."

"That must have been an awfully turbulent experience but you graduated summa cum laude from this fine establishment, you have surely settled down."

Professor Hisenryzer, brilliant as he is, has a markedly poor theory of mind.

"The dust never settles. What starts out as survival becomes a way of life. In the past year, the farthest I travelled was to one of Africa's cities of gold, south of here. Like all her sisters, she had me check my first language at the door, because if you rid a man of his mother tongue, what lullaby will he fall asleep to when your house gets cold and lonely? My stay was brief but it was not hard to find some places where the glitter was hidden."

Mr. Wabachei leaned out of his chair, slightly, and stared into an empty glass on the table.

"If you run into an old friend at a bar, briefly compare the grip in your hands and you come out the stronger, you will still be considered a baby for being in a bar with pockets full of mangangajane that nkhono gave you as mofao. How I know this is irrelevant, and all I am saying is that some places will reduce one to ridicule along with the labour of their distant relatives. But I digress."

He repositioned himself again.

The audience watched on intently and at this point, I had had two full bites of my fruit.

"I spent my last evening there with my close friend, Akofoathe 'Mpho' Chasiyabo, overlooking an airport runway, ice cream melting. Akofoathe and I grew up together. We were just kids when it happened. When tribes had a falling out, when war pared the weakest from the thick of the brave and had them flee, it came gyrating violently through our village gates. The battlefield turned bloody. The screams of the living got louder and louder still as our people joined Abel's song.

"Akofoathe's family and mine were among those who fled. We rediscovered home down south, but they soon left to pursue a better life elsewhere. Our generation grew up to eventually be scattered apart and I had lost him to the wind. No one could miss his fascination with planes; the occasional flame and smoke of the first kiss of landing, the taking off without looking back like war, the tediousness and relentless splendour of it.

"I did not have to ask. I understood his attraction immediately because, if anything, exiles find comfort flirting with the quickest exit point lest conflict get a second round. He could have gone the whole night talking about aviation nomenclature and the prim uniforms of air hostesses. But as we sat there, reminiscing our way into the early hours of a winter night, the brute landscape of tarmac below us beginning to take on a new and welcomed subtlety under glowing lights, I remembered our old primary school with shifting discomfort and remembered too the flight of our own paper planes."

"Were you two close before the war?" the professor asked, but his question went unanswered.

"The following morning, I set off for his workplace to bid him kamoso. I met him en route, bound for work himself, and we walked there together. On our way, we met a blind man whose speech had picked up where his sight had left off. He called out in joyous laughter when he heard Akofoathe's voice coming in his direction, 'Mpho! Quoi de neuf jeune homme? Tu te caches où?' There was a beauty about him, and the newspaper he had in his hand might have also added to this.

"He had his back against a signpost and his battered white cane rested compactly on the pale bricks that claimed the side of the road. 'Lumela ntate Albert!' Akofoathe replied merrily as we drew closer to him, 'U phela joang?' he asked with a tinge of concern, and slipped something into an old soda tin the man had in front him. 'Re sa phela mora,' the old man said as we walked away from his spot on the pavement. We were some distance away from him when he shouted a warning about recent attacks in the area, 'Le itlhokomele! Mpho! Ba re ho s'ona le mabaeda a emelang batho bosiu pela lijong mane ha Alisi!' 'Kea leboha ntate Albert! U hl'o itloaetse ho tsamaha ka nako u se ke oa oela kotsing!' Akofoathe shouted back in shared concern as we disappeared into the crowd.

"He smiled for a moment and told me that Albert is always picking up new phrases from travellers that give him alms. 'He has an ear for languages,' Akofoathe remarked, 'I started teaching him Sesotho just a few months ago but I bet you couldn't even tell by his accent. But it gets frustrating at times,' he said. Before I could reply, he went on, 'Just last week, I had somewhere to go and had little time to get there so I had to cut our conversation short,' Akofoathe became animated and started gesticulating, 'and when I stood up abruptly to leave, Al exclaimed,' he threw his hands dramatically in the air, "Na wetti! Wusa you di go?" 'I just left!' 'I didn't have the energy to ask or explain! I just left!' he iterated, and we broke into laughter."

He stopped and waited for the laughter of the audience to subside.

"When we arrived at his place of business, Akofoathe proceeded to tell me to whom I should give his love back in the north, if ever I found myself there again, and I bid him give Nawondinanelo my kindest regards. Meanwhile, a man arrived and ordered coffee with milk and two sweeteners. The coffee was then brought to him swiftly in exchange for some money, some of which I was made to believe was a tip. He lit a cig and then sipped his morning self into the picture.

"He greeted us cheerfully, walked over, and we were soon talking, absorbing one another through a range of discourse. Now on his third smoke, he told us that he struggles with cigarettes and the love of God. He believed in God alright, but loved how eternal smoke felt as it passed through and filled him; in and slowly out, in, and ever so slowly, out. We discussed Scripture until we had to part ways. The morning was much warmer when I left."

"You are clearly very intelligent and exceptionally well-travelled, Mr. Wabachei," remarked Professor Hisenryzer. "If I may, I am sure that a lot of ladies in this room are dying to know if you are currently seeing someone."

I took another bite as giggles rose in the room. Mr Wabachei remained unmoved.

"I am not a very cultured fellow. I have learned just enough etiquette to survive supermarket security guards and the rifles they carry gallantly under their arms, like they had one shot at groceries and decided to make it last. So to the urban folk, I am not the cream of the crop, but the bitterness that settles on the quagmire of forsakenness at the bottom. I do things differently. I was raised among the Basotho and our New Year began with an adjective, but that is for another day.

"Is love this common counterfeit you practice? Is the 'first give a strange lady your love and expect her to return it with some interest in you' any kind of love at all? In your culture, do you marry for love? Or do you marry out of reasonable doubt? I have been told that women want a red-blooded man but none whose colour keeps switching between shades of ruby and rage. Some men's love is kamikaze and you would wonder why some ladies still want a hit.

"These men break their hearts until they believe that when it comes to a loving home, they should rather find themselves a nice garden gnome to stay with. But there is hope for us all. I consider myself blessed for the method to my madness has been revised. When I was much younger, I had a friend to whose looks I was drawn, but I could not call her cute because I was afraid that words can slay and that bubbles die young. A lot of ladies I meet nowadays seem to be crazy about light skin and I personally think I am not dark enough, so it becomes difficult to win when I rely on my own wits.

"Abuse is real. If in your lover's hand their favourite card is mortal blow, do not pour down your liquor for your gods or in remembrance of the last temple they bruised. A calloused soul would do much for care and a bit of love, and this includes taking chances with the fatal gentility of noosed scarves. And desperation is also real. When one is lit aboil with passion, it becomes hard for them to remember the discomfort that accompanied the last fever. Which is worth the chase between love with and love without clipped wings? I have had plenty of lessons to learn when it comes to love. They say the sadness of love that blossoms on its own is cloudless rain that wilts and calls barrenness unto itself, but love is always love unto itself."

He slowed down for a moment and directed his expressionless face at the audience.

"When you have turned the bench you are sitting on into a faint sounding drum and you are beating at it merrily while you wait for a friend to lock up his shop in a busy street, and two women walk past you, play on. If one of these women is a lady you loved, even if it were only in retrospect, and she has since gotten married and the other is someone you would call an older friend or at least her sister in law, and they walk closely past you three times without ever saying a word, play on. If it looks like the lady you loved is a third of the curious instances into disclosing all your history together, and it starts to feel like the vultures are circling, play on. You have probably missed enough since you summoned each other's love, this time, do not skip a beat."

Mr. Wabachei adjusted his sitting position to face his interviewer, stretched his thumb and index finger from the base of his chin to his temple and started speaking in a sombre tone. The professor must have, at some point during this interview, realised that he was out of his depth.

"The trouble with unconfessed love is the telepathic expectations it comes with, such as back then, when Eleanor and I would fit together, but left our feelings unsaid. I reckoned I loved her because when we talked, I stopped feeling the ground beneath me and when we met, she would fix her eyes upon me tenderly when she thought I was not looking, even if we were in the middle of the road, faced with the menacing charge of oncoming traffic, trying desperately to cross and reach the other side with our lives intact. And when we parted ways, she would move that we embrace, especially on her father's birthday.

"Philip always said I over-think things, but Eleanor had often told me that she was not looking for love, or to be loved by anyone other than family, or for a man to call her own, so when I fell, I knew the expense would be incalculable. The problem was my leaving her when she wanted me to stay and my coming back when she least expected it, until one day she considered me dead to her like mist to the expanding warmth of morning. This was the first time I had to learn to become and be unloved. Without sounding rude or facetious, she always rejected my apologies."

He turned to the audience once more.

"During my short stay in the golden city, I desperately wanted to meet Nawondinanelo, Akofoathe's cousin. In fact, she was half the reason I was there. She was my childhood sweetheart, all until the Chasiyabos left the country. Her beauty is unrivalled. I was still very young the first time she and I talked. She would sometimes ask me to keep safe, like she would almost immediately into my hands commit her life, expecting me to traverse the treacherous space between where she was and where she needed to be in life. As safe as a hiding place she wanted me to be. I used to tell her that I loved her but when she said it back, I had to open a book about it. I wanted to know how come. For me, her name was parable condensed and retold and I had to count my blessings each time I called her.

"A collage of pictures she once sent me from abroad had me searching for words I had never learned before. It took me a short while to learn how to trace my version of perfection out of her. I thought God had me in mind when He made her. I like all the languages she speaks that might divide us but more so how I think I can always tell what she is saying when I look into her almond eyes. Keeping in touch had become a struggle that gnawed at the very fibres of my being, but I managed to get a hold of her, told her that I will be coming and that I would like to see her. She agreed to meet. I love Nawondinanelo like family, and on some days, I loved her better than her uncle did. When she left, I had to love her from afar. I figured that sometimes you have to stand a few feet away to see a flower blossom and unfold."

"She sounds remarkably lovely!" exclaimed professor Hisenryzer and Mr Wabachei gave him a sure nod.

"After Eleanor, I knew better than to love a lady sub rosa so I got Akofoathe's blessing to hold her hand when we finally met. It would be smooth sailing. She would see the mast of my eagerness approaching triumphantly in the distance and she would know that I had left my island to find her. But, alas, on the day, she had other matters to attend to, and none included me.

"The first time I got her on the phone after my trip, my first word was 'Neo?' and she just leapt at the sound of my voice, and then paused. 'Eric?' she asked calmly, 'Is that you?' I guess my question was answered and that I still had the gift of making her smile. I said, 'Yes, love. How are you? How's the family?' We talked for hours and right before the end of our conversation she says, 'Hey, listen, I'm planning to visit. I'll be there soon, okay?' 'Alright,' I said, and we hung up. I then took a deep breath and started pacing back and forth for a moment, mumbling senselessly in excitement; time to tally my blessings again. Months have passed."

A man at the back of the room gave a signal and the professor nodded in confirmation.

"Mr. Wabachei, we will have to hold it there. Thank you ever so much for taking your time to join us. Ladies and gentlemen, we have to take a break, but we will be back in ten minutes for the Q&A."

Sighs of disappointment were heard across the room. Mr. Wabachei's countenance changed again.

As I walked out of the restaurant, a brown apple in my hand, I saw Donavan, one of the waiters, still in his crisp uniform, standing on the threshold of one of the doors marked "Staff Only", looking in, the door half-closed. I walked over to him and realised that he was watching a re-run of the Africa Day ceremony. A bright graphic slid in at the bottom of a television screen, "Eric Ofeng Wabachei, Keynote Speaker, 25th May, Africa Day."

"How much do these go for, again?" I asked the fruit merchant.

"3 smoonarus each! 1 jarvas on a double."

Then Mr. Wabachei gave his speech,

> "My grandfather, my mother and I were estranged travellers. They did the distance and I found the shortest way to dirty clothes. 'A nation is whatever remnant we've got,' he would whisper to me when loneliness started closing in on me. They let me keep friends they could not see just so I survived the wilderness. The severed half of my identity I had left in the mercy of my conqueror's scribe, he who has gained the ability to whisk my emotions with a flick of the wrist. Boy without country, I asked the soil of my path to raise me like seed and it obliged but forgot to

mention that it would later claim my grandfather as payment. True, war is a pernicious affair, though from it I have learned to fight my vendetta on bloody knees. But sometimes, I wear my past like a salty wound. The Lord calls me to forgive continually.

"My kind learned the concept of pilgrimage from a very young age. We did not cease yearning to be lifted up on our fathers' shoulders like the native kids next door, but we grew up ever so accustomed to our mothers' weary backs. For us, the standard of living is set very high or very low depending on how much nurturing we managed to receive. We still have to outlive imprisonment, and the life expectancy, just to prove that our folks have raised us well. The best among us, their parents have worn out sand paper arms.

"There is no cure for homesickness in this new land I live in. I would stand for the wrong reasons if you call my name right. Eric among friends, Ofeng Wabachei among kin, but Heaven recognises the real me despite all my pseudonyms, spots me below any star under which I lay my head upon rocks. I have become a master at reading labels. Mine is bold. It says 'co-heir' but many confuse the word with 'foreigner.' What you call 'outsider' comes from deep within you, just like ill humour intends, remember that you too have been crafted in. Will you continue to call unholy what God has cleansed?

"I have lived in three different countries and have seen many more. It is yet to be explained to me how townships can set sail when their dreams are branded old yawns. We lone souls like to walk our shadows round the block now and again just to pause life and reflect, but all thinking caps come off come night-time, lest you be mistaken for something you are not; something like a predator, or something like a willing victim. All roads must lead to a pile of bricks and sheets of metal one happens to call home at night-time. But of course, unless one is a street capitalist, a neighbourhood profiteer whose work shift starts a few spliffs after the clock has hit dusk.

"These you will find in different sizes and in an assortment of colours from a brittle and calculating man who negotiates best behind a blade's edge to a woman who has applied enough wit to her trade to realise that any spaza shop can double up as a make-shift convenience for a quick transaction. But our environment hugs us all the same and will not let us go. The very darkness that lays beyond our curtains looks for a place to rest, but it is to light we give lodging. So we are in motion only when sunlight starts to lick our dusty roads. Yet something as precious as us, we continue to fall with the blazing sun.

"Many in poverty confuse the word for work with the experience of burden. We are no strangers to those who work to the end of their bodies to earn a break. The growth of their children they miss, the child they miss and wonder how quickly time passes by – it was only last night when they tucked them into bed and they still had that new baby smell. Our prayers are without end for the little ones.

"A lot of people have contributed immensely to my life but their contribution alone is salad for the Greeks. To remember them only for their contribution would be a sacrilege of their love. It is on account of their grace towards me that I am able to speak to you today; that I ask on whose side we really are if we sell perfume to a people whose dire need is the fragrance light summer rains infuse into the air? Of what end is humility when we mix our pride with bitter herbs?

"Some of the worst politics I have heard is words that keep wells of tears bound. Soon there will not be any shoulders left to cry on, the way they have the people divided. Malice will always take root in fallow hearts so be clear about the fruit you want to reap when you divorce your men from emotion and reserve tears for woman and child. There is little wonder why they gradually become so cold and unfeeling. Their grogginess is a funnel taking back what it has worked for.

"Let your opinions be derivatives of truth. When you are in the way of truth, do you beg it remains with you or beg it takes you with? Having fled your own country will teach you that regardless of the perceived need, it is manipulation to try to wear down the Lord with prayer and sulking for Him to submit to your own will. Turmoil does not render it possible to please Him without faith. Mud and spit is saliva and the soil of our death only in the hands of common men. Smile, even if the things that brighten your mood are yet minute for the unkind to notice. Swallow your breathing awhile and then pray for the men among you who bow to God pretentiously like the dip of the willows. Ladies and gentlemen, allow me to ask, 'Who is your neighbour?'

"The most joyous and boldest words I can ever say out loud and with sheer resolve are, "Almighty, Triune God." We were made from the soil of God's Word and took the form and formlessness of spirit, body and soul. Do not forget how they sought out the Lord for thirty pieces of silver. Remember that for us He was freely given as sacrifice. When the Holy Spirit in you addresses your relationship with sin, you cannot fail to notice that sins of self and body sully the whole being. Confess your sins continually. If you become hated and reviled and the Lord delivers you from those who persecute you, know that it is not the end of the tunnel; the light belongs to the fourth man in the furnace."

Donavan slammed the door, leaving behind him a reverberating sound of colliding wood and metal, and walked right past me without saying a word.

"Young man!" yelled the merchant, enraged. "All I asked was why you were buying another apple when you still have one in your hand!"

"And what I'm telling you is that I don't particularly like brown apples!" I shouted back.

"Go ahead then, pick one! Go on, or simply get lost!" replied the man, and gave a rude gesture.

I did not flinch however. I paused for a moment, and then started prodding my fingers against a stack of apples in silence.

By now, evening had come. Some men stood near their stalls and fed wood and cardboard boxes to crackling flames for warmth. Candles and solar-powered lamps dotted the market place and clearance sales on perishables had started at vegetable stands. Through the brisk winter air, a jangling sound of keys was heard as some vendors started to clear their treasured booths and pack up. Night slowly crept in.

Kamora Setsokotsane

'Masello Constancia Sello

Ho lehlohonolo bohle ba nang le mofuthu oa lerato la lelapa. Bohle ba tsebang moo ba sunyang 'hlooho tsa bona teng hole joang kapa joang, ebile ba tseba hore hona le batho ba ba emeng nokeng ka linako tsohle.

Liako o holetse lelapeng le hlokang mofuthu oa lerato, o ne a phela le motsoali a le mong feela, 'me a sa tsebe moo e mong a leng teng. Kamehla o ne a lakatsa eka lelapa lab'o le kabe le felletse joaloka malapa a'bo lithaka tsa hae tse ling, hoo ebile a neng a le mona. 'Maliako o ne a mo omanya letsatsi le chabang le le likelang, hosena mohlang a mo thabelang joalo-ka morali oa hae. Kamano ena e ile ea fetola Liako ngoana a lulang a hlorile, a sitoang ho etsa metsoalle. Liako o'na boetse a kena skolo ka bohase, a ea ka liphahlo tse litšila le lieta tse tabohileng hoo metsi a neng a kena ha pula ena. Ruri e ne e le lesea le sa ratoeng, e ne e ka ke ngoana ea senang hab'o.

Liako o ne a shebahala e le ngoana ea bohlale sekolong empa ka lebaka la khotso eo a neng a e hloka, o ne a sa sebetse ka mokhoa o khahisang matichere a hae. Ha lilemo li ntse li ea, matichere a hae a ne a leka tsohle ho bua le eena ho utloa mathata a hae empa o ne a sa re letho. 'Maliako le eena o ne a bitsoe, a botsoa lipotso empa eena a halefa ka le reng matichere aa bona hore ngoanana o hlooho e thata. Lipuo tsa hae li ne li elellisoe matichere ao hore mohlomong bothata bo ka lapeng. Ka botho, ba ne ba leke ho atamela 'Maliako empa o ne a halefa le hofeta a ba a ntša ngoana sekolong. Lebaka la hae e ne e le hore mosebetsi oa matichere ke ho ruta eseng ho shebana le litaba tsa lelapa la hae. Liako ha a qeta ho tsoa sekolo o ile a nka nakoana a lula hae a sa etse letho, 'me le mathata a hae eaba a ntse a eketseha hobane ho ne ho se moo a ka balehelang teng ho qoba bohale ba 'm'ae.

Liako o'na lula a ipotsa hore na o ile a siteloa 'm'ae kae kaha ho ne ho bonahala a n'a sa mo rate. E ne e le bohobe ba hae ba letsatsi hore 'm'ae a mo joetse kamoo a mo senyelitseng bophelo ka teng. Ka matsatsi a mang 'm'ae o ne a ka mo siea feela a sa mo joetsa moo a eang teng ebe o ikhutlela mohlang ho ratang eena.

Ka le leng ha a ntse a bala koranta eo a neng a phuthelletsoe bohobe ka eona shopong, Liako o n'a hlokomele khoebo e fanang ka lihlaphiso tsa ho kenya bana ba hlokang sekolo. Litaba tseo li ne li khahle Liako, 'me a khetha ho ngola kopo hang-hang hore le eena a tle a fumane monyetla. O ne a na le tšepo ha a isa lengolo leo posong, ebile a qeta le maikutlo a hae hose joetse 'm'ae hofihlela a thotse karabo. Libeke li ne li fete ka bongata a sa thole karabo eaba o fihleloa ke mohopolo oa hore mohlomong kopo ea hae e ne e latotsoe. Ho kokobetsa matšoafo, o ne a ee shopong moo mangolo a neng a posetsoa teng ho ea botsa na la hae le ne le fihle na. Liako o ne a makale haholo ha mosebetsi oa shopong moo a mo joetsa hore efela le ne le fihle eaba le nkuoa ke 'm'ae. Ka morao ho mono o ne a potlakele hae a kututsa hohle ka tlung a batlana le lengolo, a mpa a nyahama ha a sa le thole. 'Maliako ha a fihla o ne a kharumele Liako ka bohale a ba a eketsa ka hore morekisi eo oa shopong o ne a mo etselletsa. Liako o ne a kebisi hlooho, a khathala matla eaba likhapha li keleketla marameng.

'Maliako o ne a boele a mo hopotsa kamoo a mo senyelitseng bophelo ka teng: "Ke tena ke sotlehile tjena ke hloka monna ka lebaka la hau. Ntate oa hau o ne a nthata, a ntlhokomela, ebile a ntšepisitse lenyalo. Bophelo ba'ka bo ne bo le monate ke bona hore 'na le eena re tla ba 'moho ho fihlela. O ile a nlahla ha ke ba mokhachane ka uena, a nfetohela joalo'ka lempetje. Ke ea o bolella Liako, ha hona mohlang u tla phela hamonate ha feela ntse ke phela lefatšeng lena. Ke tla u senyetsa bophelo joalo'ka ha u sentse baka le 'na". Liako o ne a amohele litaba tseo a nt'o tsoa ka monyako. Ka kelellong ea hae o ne a bona hole molemo hore a mpe a ichoelle.

Ka letsatsi le leng e ne e re ha 'Maliako a tsamaile, ke ha Liako a nka monyetla. Pele o ne a nahane ho siela 'm'ae lengolo empa a fetola monahano ka la hore 'm'ae h'a lokeloe le ho sieloa letho. O ne a latele ka ho nka moqomo oa lipilisi tsa 'm'ae tsa boroko a nt'o li noa kaofela. Ho se hokae o ne a apareloe ke boroko bo matla eaba o itahlela moalong, a khaleha.

Liako o ne a tsohe a sa tsebe moo a leng teng a utloa a opeloa ke hlooho ebile a na le mokhathala o mongata. Ha a qamaka eaba o thola hore o sepetlele. Hang hoba a tsohe, ngaka a be a s'a le pel'a hae a mo shebile ka mahlong ebile a mo botsa na o ikutloa joang. Moo ba ntseng ba bua ke ha 'Maliako a kena monyako ka sefahleho se bontšang motho ea thabileng. Liako a makala hobane o ne a qala ho bona 'm'ae a thabile. Ngaka e ne e bolelle Liako kamoo 'm'ae a neng a tšoenyehile ka teng le hore o ne a hlotse a mo etetse sepetlele ho mo hloela. Liako o ne a thabe, pelo ea hae ea tlaloa ke khotso le tšepo, a lumela hore 'm'ae o ne a se a mo rata a itelletse ho fetola tsela eo a neng a mo phelisa ka eona.

Hang hoba ngaka a tsoe monyako, lebonyo la 'Maliako la ne le nyamele, a tiisetsa morali ka mahlong, a retela, eaba o botsa Liako hore na o ne a nahana o tla phonyoha habonolo hakaalo na. O ne a mo joetse hore e ne e be lehlohonolo hore o ne a hopole tuku eo a neng a e siile hae eaba o khutla tseleng ha a tla mo fumana a rapame fatše le botlolo ea lipilisi.

*

Ka morao hore a lokolloe sepetlele, bophelo ba Liako bo ile ba mpefala hofeta. 'M'ae o ne a se a lula a mo katile ka leihlo le nchocho. Liako o ne a khethe hore hang ha a folile o tla thoba hae, a itjoetsa hore a ka mpa 'lo shoella naha-thota ho'na le ho phela moo liheleng. Letsatsi leo ha le fihla o ne a nke monyetla 'm'ae a sa ile mabakeng eaba o paka ling tsa hae o betseha ka monyako. O ne a tsamae joalo letšeare kaofela, a lapile, a nyoruoe, empa a itjoetsitse hore hae teng ha se moo a khutlelang. O ne a khekhethehe joalo hofihlela a fihla tseleng e eang teropong eaba o kena koloing ea pele e emang. Koloi e ne e tsamae joalo ho fihlela e qetellong ea leeto la eona. Letsatsi le ne le se le liketse, Liako o ne a tšohile a ipotsa na o tla etsa joang. O ne a khethe ho kena motseng o mong o haufi eaba o tsamaea hofihlela lefifi le mo tšoarella tseleng. Kaha o ne a se a felletsoe ke maqheka, o ne a khethe ho ala tjale ea hae pel'a sefate eaba oa khaleha.

O ne a tsosoe ke letsoho le neng le mo sisinya lehetleng, ha a bula mahlo eaba o kopana le sefahleho sa mosali eo a neng a se a le moholo lilemong. 'M'e eo o ne a mo botse lebitso le moo a tsoang teng eaba o itsebisa e le 'Matholo, mong'a jarete eo Liako a neng a le ka har'a eona. 'Matholo o ne a meme Liako hore ba ee ka tlung ba tsebe ho bua.

'Matholo o ne a mamele litaba tsa Liako, 'me a hauoa. Kaha Liako e n e le ngoana ea ratehang, 'Matholo le monna oa hae ba ne ba lumellana horè batla mo nka a lule le bona ba be ba mo busetse sekolong. Liako o ne a phele hamonate ntle le qeaqeo ha 'Matholo, a ba a fetela sekolong sa mopheho ka morao hore a qete sekolong se phahameng. Ha a fihla lilemong tsa bokharebe, o ne a kopane le mohlankana ea bitsoang Tieho. Eo abuti o ne a khahluoe haholo hoo a ileng a potlaka a kopa Liako ho batsoali ba hae ba bacha.

'Matholo o ne a ba thabele haholo a mpa a soaba ha a bona ntate eena a sa thaba. Liako le 'Matholo ba ne ba iphapanye hobane ba ne ba nahana monna-moholo o ne a hloka nako ea ho thuisa litaba tseo.

Ka letsatsi le leng Liako o ne a iphumane a setse a le mong le ntata'e ka tlung. Ke hona moo, moo ntata'e a neng a mo tšele ka tsona a mo joetsa hore o ne a sa thabele mohlankana oa hae le hore a khaohane le eena. Liako o ne a tšohe habohloko a botsa na hobane'ng, ntata'e ke ha a halefa a mo joetsa hore a keke a mo holisa a sa tsebe le moo a neng a hlaha teng ebe monnanyana e mong oa mo nka.

E ne e re ha a cho joalo eaba o tšoara Liako o mo lietse fatše, oa mo jabela. Moo a lekang ho hoelehetsa eaba seatla sa monna-moholo se mo koala molomo. Liako o ne a leke ho raha le ho hoelehetsa empa eaba ha hona thuso. O ne a elelloe morero oa ntata'e ha a utloa liphahlo tsa hae li taboloa eaba o leka ho itoanela, empa hone hosena thuso. Liako o ne a koale mahlo a hae ka thata, a rapela hore Molimo a mo lokolle litlamong tseo tse bohloko. Ho sa le joalo, keha a utloa motho a hoelehetsang ka khalefo. Tieho o ne a tšoare ntat'a Liako, eaba o mo thulanya le lebota. O ne a phuthe Liako ba potlakela kamoreng ea hae hore a apare liphahlo tse ling, le hore ba nke lithepa tsa hae. Ha ba qetile ba leba hab'o Tieho.

Ka letsatsi le hlahlamang Liako o ne a kope hore Tieho a mo felehetse ba ee hab'o a tsebe ho tlalehela 'm'e tse etsahetseng. Ho fihleng hoa bona ba ne ba amoheloe ke 'Matholo a sa thabang, a bontšang a halefile. Liako o ne a makale ha 'Matholo a mo hlapaola a mo qosetsa ho leka ho mo utsoetsa. Liako le Tieho ba ne ba leke ho hlalosa 'nete ea se etsahetseng eaba 'Matholo ha a li kene. Bobeli boo keha bo tela, ba khutlela moo ba tsoang.

Liako o ne a hlore nako e telele ka mor'a mono hobane o ne a hopotse 'm'ae 'Matholo. O ne a itjoetse hore ho betere a amohele maemo hobane mosali-moholo o ne a sa batle ho utloa letho. 'Mali a ka inahanela ho makala hoa Liako mohlang a fumanang moloaetsa o mo joetsang ka phupu ea ntata'e le hore 'm'ae o lakatsa ho 'mona. Ho fihleng hoa hae moo, 'Matholo ke ha a mo joetsa hore monna-moholo

113

o mo joetsitse tsohle tse neng li etsahale pele a leba bo-ea-batho, 'me a kopa hore Liako a mo tšoarele. Leha ba ne ba kopantsoe ke litaba tse bohloko, Liako le 'm'ae ba ne ba keteke poelano ea bona ka ho akana nako e telele ba ntse ba bososela.

The Two

Kaizer Matsumunyane

To many they could just be two people looking for a lift. Nothing more. I thought so too. I saw them from afar and wanted to pass them. What, with all the crime in South Africa? They will find a way of getting home. I'm not their only option. There are other drivers on the road. Someone is bound to give them a lift. I hope. No, someone always does or there wouldn't be hitchhikers. Let me play some music and I will forget them. I had passed many before. I'm sure they could hear the van with its diesel engine as it approached them, but they just kept walking. They did not turn to stop it. As I was about to pass them, they turned around at the same time and waved the car down. I looked at them and I had to stop. A shrivelled old man and a younger woman. The old man was shuffling his feet. I felt something I can't explain. I slowed down the van and stopped a few metres from them. The man came running and shuffling at the same time. The woman followed him, synchronized acrobatics. I got out of the car to ask where they are going. Marquad, the old man said.

The old man looked like he had been through all the storms of life, but now they live inside him. The woman, she looked much younger than him, but you could swear they had followed each other in life and had the same beginning or the man waited in life for her to be born and then walked with her. He got in the back of the van with thankfulness. She got in the front. I started the car and tried to make small conversation with the woman. She looked at me and tried to speak, but only sound with nothing came out. She was mute. After that, she retreated into her world. I looked at the back of the van to the old man, it seemed like only he could enter her world. I drove and played music. She just stared at the road without making a sound. I kept looking at the back of the van to the old man as we drove. We arrived at Marquad. I stopped by a truck on the road and she got out. The old man tried climbing out of the van, but was having difficulty. I opened the back and he finally got out. He smiled with thankfulness. She also smiled. His last word, "Tixo," meaning God.

They have been on the road for some time. Many years. He doesn't care to count. He, shuffling his feet. She, walking besides him, carrying her silence. He is all she has. She only knows him. He knows her too. He knew others before. He had choices. He is afraid to tell her that he does not know where they are going. He only knows how to live like this. Here comes another car. He waves it down.

Epiphany

Nicole Tau

Sitting alone in my cozy apartment, wallowing in self-pity, I sense the vile smell of gas invading the dining room. Reclining on the dining room chair, looking at a half full glass of red wine... "Damn. I don't even like wine." I faintly grin.

I still attempt to concentrate and collect my thoughts in spite of how light-headed I feel, to try and go down the memory lane of my life, and discover how I got here; to understand how I contemplated taking my own life rather than living it.

And as the gas from the kitchen grows unbearable, I cling harder onto my last memories of everything I hold dear, everything that back then I thought was worth living for, and it hits me; are all my problems worth dying for?

*

"Bonang, I need all these files ready tomorrow morning by 9 am sharp," said Mr. Bongani, my boss, as he dumped a huge stack of papers on my desk before waddling off into his office.

Already drained from the strenuous day at work and constant complaints from clients at the law firm I worked in, all I could do was go through the documents like a zombie, wishing for a weekend, and it was only Tuesday...

Let's just say being a glorified secretary of an obnoxious attorney was not the job I had dreamed of. But when most of my tuition fees got spent by my alcoholic father on his rehabilitation centres and lawsuits, there was no choice but to drop out of law school and find other ways to make it in life.

So I ended up working for a pit bull of a boss, as I like to call him, and shared my apartment with a girl I suspected was on drugs, but hey, she helped with the rent and as the saying goes; beggars can't be choosers.

Yet for a while, somehow, I still had dreams and ambitions; had been saving up for university for years; had sacrificed my social life and dating. Sad, but my dreams of one day becoming a successful attorney had seemed to be worth sacrificing for. However, when weeks turned into months, months into years...dreaming became much harder.

As I was buried in mountains of files and documents, a pleasant cologne scent hit my nose. Looking up curiously through my thick glasses, my jaw fell slightly open at the sight of the finest specimen of a man I had ever seen walk onto our floor.

Tall and well-tanned, he had short curly hair and dark brown eyes, kind of like mine, but less expressive and way more intense. *There is no way he was from around here*, I had thought to myself. I even fancied touching him to see if he was not just a mirage from my long day at work.

"Um, how may I help you Sir?" I managed to pull up my jaw into an automatic polite smile, praying to gods and heavens my cheeks were not as flushed as they felt.

The man in front of me, in a sharp tailored navy blue suit, regarded me amused; a certain, unexplained spark playing in his eyes. I was not sure if it was my curly hair, which had looked better in the magazine, or the ugly gray suit I had chosen to wear that morning.

"I'm here for the appointment with Mr. Bongani, please." He flashed a smile that got my feet all wobbly and for the first time ever, I thanked my stiff chair for the support.

Mastering all the strength I could from my body, I rose from my seat to extend my slightly trembling hand to him, which he clasped warmly. "I don't think I got your name, Sir..." I asked, regaining some of my already lacking self-esteem.

"My goodness! How foolish of me. I'm Mr. Stephens, director of an architecture firm in London, England," said Mr. Stephens, slightly embarrassed.

Becoming at ease, I smiled warmly at him to not blush at his ridiculously adorable British accent.

"Bring him in!" barked Mr. Bongani through the phone receiver.

After showing Mr. Stephens in, he bowed slightly to me and departed through the double doors.

As I sat there day dreaming, curling a lock of my hair around my finger, a familiar heel-clacking noise brought me back to reality.

"Hey sis!" My younger sister, Posh, announced herself uninvited as usual, balancing her three year old daughter, Kenya, on one arm and shopping bags on the other.

Cringing at her annoying voice, I shushed her with a finger. "My boss is in a very important meeting, Posh! What the heck are you doing here with Kenya?" I gestured at my three year-old niece, although I couldn't help but smile pleasantly at the little bundle of joy.

"Jeez, you on PMS or something?!" Popping her gum, Posh sat Kenya on my desk. "Anyway, I know you're busy and all, but I really have to go somewhere important and I can't take Kenya with me...you'll look after her right?"

Posh, was halfway into her magic trick of disappearing, and leaving me dumbfounded, when she spun around, grinning wildly. "And oh, I reeeeaally need R500 for a new weave." Patting her scalp softly, "this weave is driving me crazy yoh," she said.

In a delayed reaction, I clasped my hands tight and bristled.

"Posh! You cannot just leave Kenya with me like this unexpectedly, at my work," I pleaded, but whispering harshly so as not to be heard by my boss.

"I am tired Posh!"

Letting out a short laugh in sarcasm, Posh narrowed her eyes at me. "You, tired? Sis, you aren't the one who gave birth at seventeen and don't have a job. You got it easy while it's hard enough for me just to get by... "

Glaring at Posh in disbelief, I had almost laughed hysterically.

"You are a piece of work! Posh, you're almost turning twenty-one, and you never even attempted to have a job, while I, and anyone you could manipulate, have kept looking after you and your child without receiving even the slightest gesture of gratitude. You are the one who ran away when Mom fell sick, and didn't even show up at her funeral...and you didn't have to face Dad; miserable, drowning himself in liquor every single day..." I paused, controlling my temper.

Posh seemed to have lost her tongue.

"Okay. Chill! You could have just said that you're tied up or something, jeez! No need to lose it in front of the kid," said Posh, clearly taken aback.

Hoisting Kenya back into her arms, Posh stormed away without saying another word, her heels clacking away fiercely on the ceramic floor.

Taking a breath of relief that the scene did not cause any more chaos, I was about to sit down when Mr. Bongani's door opened and Mr. Stephens walked out, preceded by Mr. Bongani.

"I will certainly try my best to make it, Sir. Quite frankly however, I just want to get past the lawsuit. It has already consumed a lot of my time, as you may imagine," said Mr. Stephens dryly.

Mr. Bongani brushed away the issue with a simple wave of a hand.

"Ah, do not worry about that. Consider the matter solved. We've got some of the finest attorneys in the land!"

Catching me observing them, Mr. Stephens turned his attention to me.

"And I genuinely commend you Sir on your company's great staff."

Turning around, as though seeing me there for the first time, Mr. Bongani adjusted his suit with pride.

"Well thank you Mr. Stephens, we do strive for excellence. This is Ms. Khumalo, eh... Bonang. She is an invaluable asset to our company."

Raising my eyebrow at Mr. Bongani in amusement, I almost snorted, but managed to maintain my composure burying myself in documents; the less I saw of the pit bull, the better.

Mr. Stephens seemed to have noticed my way of keeping my opinions to myself.

"It was truthfully, nice meeting you Ms. Khumalo," an enigmatic smile playing on his lips. Turning to Mr. Bongani, Mr. Stephens bowed slightly, "I will see you on Thursday Mr. Bongani." With that he departed from us, leaving me somehow subdued.

As I got home, my heart skipped a beat at finding the front door knob broken.

Cautiously entering the apartment I called out to my roommate, but only echo answered me back. So, mustering all my courage, I turned the lights on and my fears were confirmed. My roommate's belongings were gone and so were my television set, sound system, microwave and possessions that no amount of money could replace. Those included my late mother's chinaware, my grandmother's silver cutlery set and the Persian rug I had gotten for my housewarming.

More calm than I should have been, I shuffled over to the couch and just laid there, exhausted, staring at the ceiling for a long time, before finally calling the police and narrating the whole incident.

The rest of the week passed as though it were a blur. My boss barked at me a few times, some clients cried, some laughed and some simply looked like they had eaten something unpleasantly bitter.

Then on one very ordinary Monday, something extraordinary happened.

"Would you fancy yourself having lunch with me, Ms. Khumalo?" I heard a familiar voice say. Looking up, Mr. Stephens stood before me in all his majesties. Not expecting the question and also taken by surprise, I took a minute too long to answer.

"Um, well… no, I mean, yes. Lunch? Sure…" I stuttered, "We all have to eat at some point." That was my poor attempt at making a joke, but if I had seen correctly through my thick glasses, to my pleasure, Mr. Stephens let out a sigh of relief.

As it turned out at lunch, Mr. Stephens had a decent sense of humor and was quite a well-travelled man. But what was more interesting was that he was interested in me, and we had so much in common. I was pinching myself like crazy the entire lunch, just to make sure I was not dreaming.

That one lunch turned into many more outings, filled with laughter, joy and a feeling of complacency that everything was falling into place at long last in my life. My subconscious bubbled in delight at the thought that maybe, this fine specimen of a man was my ticket out of the Cookoo town that I had allowed my family to create for me. We went for lunch every other day, dined at expensive, candle lit restaurants and went on adventurous short trips to see caves, and to hike and camp by the banks of rivers. All this went on for few wonder-filled weeks, until just as it had begun spontaneously, so it ended.

"I have to go back, to London love, in three days." He said casually, avoiding eye contact with me.

My face fell, just as the words out of his beautiful mouth.

"Then why this?" I gestured around, feeling myself getting upset.

"I just knew that I had to be with you. I didn't think time would fly by so quickly. Please understand..." Mr. Stephens seemed to be at a loss for words, but I just could not entertain that.

"Understand what, exactly? That you actually had no intentions with me? Mr. Stephens, I am not the type of a person who constantly goes on dates... I do not have that kind of time luxury. When I go out, I make it a meaningful date... and from what I deduct now, I am nothing but another of your African experiences!"

Mr. Stephens seemed to be confused, "No... it is nothing like that. Calm down... How would you ever know that the date is meaningful if you hardly even go out? I did not mean to lead you on so much; I honestly thought that we were great company to each other and that both of us could use a break from work."

I knew I was overreacting, and in another life I would have brushed it all away, but my life was complicated enough. I felt angry that I always had to work twice as hard as other people to get what I want, to achieve even a tinge of what happiness feels like.

"Mr. Stephens… Frankly, I do not have time for pointless dates; I have other priorities. And since you had no intentions with arousing my feelings, then I suppose for future reference, you should try picking the great company of a suburban Barbie."

Paying for the coffee, I rose from my seat, "Goodbye Mr. Stephens," and walked away before he could see tears of disappointment welling in my eyes.

Back in my empty apartment, I looked around and felt as lonely as ever. Suddenly, everything seemed pointless and grey.

As I was getting out of my working clothes, the emptiness of my apartment was filled with a phone call.

"Yes?" I answered, uninterested.

"Yeah… Um, hey sis… So, I need you to bail me out… Kind of got busted for some stuff… Long story," said Posh, popping her unnerving chewing gum through the receiver.

Massaging one of my temples, I almost hung up. "Did you at least ask Dad to help you, or one of your boyfriends?"

"Jeez, would I be calling you if I could do that?! Dad left rehab again… from what I heard, he could be facing charges for drunk driving… And KB got arrested two weeks back. As for Kenya's dad, I heard he got deported." Posh paused, "Anyway, the officer here is looking at me crazy. So you'll bail me right?!" With that, Posh hung up.

Letting out a dry laugh, I leaned against the wall and closed my eyes.

*

As extreme fatigue envelops my body, my will to live suddenly kicks in. I realize that I honestly do not want to die…

123

Sprawled out on the table with the glass of wine still half full, I push myself up. *"Damn, why is the kitchen so far all of a sudden?"* I think to myself as my will starts to abandon me.

In my poor attempt to reach the kitchen stove some inches away, I powerlessly drop to the floor as my mind begins to blank out. All I can feel is the coldness of the ceramic floor filling my flesh and feeding my feeling of solitude. As a tear trickles down my cheek, I hear my front door open and that familiar British voice calling out for me. "Ms. Khumalo... Bonang?"

Through heavy eyelids, I can see him... My fine specimen kneeling down before me. "Mr. Stephens..." is all I can whisper before everything fades.

Bophelo bo naka li maripa

Litšoanelo **Nei**

"U tla llela metsotso ngoan'ake, ke bona u potlakile haholo". Ke mantsoe a nkhono ao. Homme a sa hlokofala hee mofokeng eo ke ketso tsaka tsa bocheng. E se feela, nkile ka nkuoa ke lefatše ke tletsoe ke boikhantšo, ke lumela hore ha ho poho-peli, poho ke 'na feela! Ke ne ke holisoa ke eena nkhono, ke le ntho e ka matsohong ke sa hloke letho. Eare ha ke kena boroetsaneng ka fetoha tuu ka makatsa ba bangata ba neng ba ntšepile.

Ea re likolo li phomoletse keresemese, hoa fihla motseng mohlankana oa seithati a tsoa Belekomo. E mochitja ea litšika-tšika,a tsamaea ka boqhetseke bohle, pono e ntle ruri. Ka hanong teng e le kheleke. Khele! ka lumela ho nkeha maikutlo ke eena, etsoe o ile a nkatamela boo! Ra tšepisana maholimo le mafatše hoo ke ileng ka utloa hore sekolo se tla salla ba se ratang, ha e le 'na ke ne ke sala tjaka eo morao. Re ile ra rera ho tsoa ka la pholo-khoaba. Nkhono a qhoeloa habohloko ke taba eo, hoo a neng a kene sepetlele ke pelo bohloko.

Ke ne ke sa natse letho, maikutlo a hapehile ke koete. Bo-malome ba lekile ho nthiba empa ka ba tšetlehela mabaka ka boikhohomoso bohle hofihlela ba liha melala. Ka letsatsi le behiloeng ra fela ra kena tseleng. Hlathe e lelekisa tsebe ka hore ke ne ke qala ho tsoa ka har'a motse oa heso oa Linakeng. Leeto la ntšulafalla hanyane ha re palama bese e lebang Belekomo, basali lehlatso! Eabe e fofa le eona, empa ea re pepa ka botšepehi ra ba ra re kutu! lekeisheneng. Ao! Ka tloaela kapele, ka nonopela. Ra phela hamonate le eo molekane oaka, eo ke neng ke 'mitsa Ati Jemese. Joale ebe o tla bobotheha hamonatjana a bolele kamoo ke leng lehakoe la pelo ea hae kateng. Ke ne ke lebetse tuu ka ba 'lapa leso, ke ja monakalali oa keboleloa. Nako ea feta, meso ea tsoala mesoana; ka le leng ka elelloa hore ke 'meleng. Ka emela Ati

Jemese hore a khutle mosebetsing hore a tlo utloa taba tsena tse monate.

"Letekatse tooe!": Ke eena eo, "'na kea sebetsa uena u tlala-tlala le motse u ntlisetsa likhohloana?" Ha a rialo a ntjabela haholo ka mpama ka ba ka bona linaleli. Ka ea bobeli teng ka hla ka ilibana. Ha ke re phapha ka fumana ke le sepetlele,'mele oaka o choachoasela, hlooho e le boima. Mooki ea neng a nhlahloba a nkeletsa hore ke leke ho phomola kaha ke lahlehetsoe ke mali a mangata, 'moho le leseanyana laka. Ke ile ka sareloa haholo, le ho utloa hore Ati Jemese haa ka a le beha sepetlele. Baoki bao ba molemo ba ile ba nhlabolla ka makhethe, 'me ka ikana hore le 'na ke tla fetola maphelo a batho.

E bile tšoabo e kholo ha ke kena motseng haeso ke hoshola ke tšaba ho teanya mahlo le batho. Semomotela sane sa phokeng se phobetse habohloko, tšobotsi li qhalane. Nkhono a nkamohela ka meokho empa a nkhothatsa, a ntlhokomela, 'me ka okoloha ka boela ka ba motho hape! Ke ile ka boela sekolong moo ke ileng ka ithukhubetsa ka setotsoana hofihlela ke qeta lithuto tsaka tsa booki. Ke nakong eo moo ke ileng ka hlohonolofatsoa ka lerato la sebele, ka qetella ke nyaloa ke ngaka e kholo sepetleleng seo ke neng ke sebetsa ho sona. Nkhono o n'a hlabe o bohale molilietsane mohla lechato laka, le bo-malome lifahleho li elile.

Nako e ile ea feta, lelapa laka la tiea ra sitsoa ka poropotloana tse tharo tse masene. Thabo e kholo ruri. Ka tsatsi le leng ha ke le mosebetsing ke ha ke re ptjang-ptjang le sefahleho seo ke neng ke se ke se lebetse. Pono e nyarosang ruri! Leha a ne a se a phobetse, a reketla ha a tsamaea, kahla ka bona ka tseka la mathe; lona lane la ho nkhapa maikutlo mehleng, hore enoa ke Ati Jemese. Marama a ne a bothetse, 'tlalo le borethe lane le qhitsa lihloba, mahlo a le masehla, melomo e rephile e le lilatsoa. Re ile ra shebana kahar'a thaka tsa mahlo, eaba o re sihla! Fatše. Re ile ra mo phalla ka potlako le basebetsi 'moho le 'na, 'me kajeno ke mokuli oaka ea hlabolohileng ea seng a amohetse hore o tla phela ka kokoana-hloko ea bosolla-hlapi.

Ba ile ba bua Basotho, ba re: "bophelo bo naka li maripa."

The Gifts

Lipuo Motene

He lies on his bed, tossing and turning, enduring helplessly the excruciating pain that seems to wrack his whole body. Life has lost all meaning for him. There is no beginning, no end. Days and nights flow into one another in a seamless wearisome rhythm. His life is taking a distinct downward curve. It is falling apart. In an attempt to speak, Taelo's voice is weak, filled with wistful nostalgia, he begins, "Matau and my sons, in this world, I have caused sufferings, I have wronged my gods. My sins are like scarlet. But now if I learn to do right, they will be as white as snow."

His wife and two sons, Tokelo and Limpho, all sit in silence, unmoved but very expectant, listening keenly and hanging on every word he is uttering. Taelo continues, "As you can all see, my days are numbered on earth, I'm going to die, but I want to go home with a clear conscience. This is why I'm asking for forgiveness in all the wrong things I have done to you. But most importantly, I need you to help me organize a ceremony of *Boipeletso*, I need to be cleansed to appease my ancestors. I want to ask for their forgiveness, I have wronged them in all imaginable ways. I need Ntate Mosika here tomorrow, I need him very much. I also need my relatives. I'm going to tell everyone that I am tired of fighting, I'm now prepared to do the right thing. But because the three of you are very close to me, I feel compelled to tell you first."

There is an almost eerie sense of remoteness in Taelo's eyes, he is lost in deep introspect, he has retreated deep inside himself to a different place, a different time, far from this cold brutal world he is trapped in. He is travelling through the rocky roads of his times. Thoughts about his past conjure up a tumbling kaleidoscope of bittersweet memories.

*

"Ntate, the car is ready, says Tokelo. He is driving Taelo to a business meeting where he is going to sign a 2 million Maluti tender. The lucrative businesses he owns merely serve to give a surface explanation to the wealth he has acquired. In reality, much of his businesses are not flattering as he is a leader of a vicious crew of sadistic gangsters who undertake underground activities.

Taelo sits in his living room casually going through the pages of a newspaper. His only concern in the papers is the business world as an influential businessman, a man who is also at heart a family man. Some people however describe him as a two-faced ferocious tycoon who would do anything to make it to the top, even if it means going on a killing spree. His eyes catch a glimpse of a headline which immediately grabs his attention. The caption reads, "No Graceful Way Out This Time for Mr. Tokelo aka the Fish," the article reads. "This time it is an open-and-shut case as the Fish was caught red handed in possession of mutilated body parts. This is a man, who has been indicted and tried several times with cases ranging from ritual killings, corruption and hijacking, but always manages to walk away free. This time the state has made his case a high profile one. The evidence against him is irrefutable as he is as guilty as Cain."

Halfway through the article, a look of desperation comes over his face and he is engulfed in a red mist of terror. "I hate this press! Why are they poking their noses in everything? They are making matters even worse." His wife rushes in, "Ntate, what is it now?" Taelo retorts, "It's this press again, I don't see any chance of making it through this time." Matau responds, "Ntate don't start, this is just one of those annoying stories, if we managed to convince them to give you bail, you know we will always find a way out." Indeed, no one knew how he did it. To many it is as though the law is making exceptions when dealing with him. He is indeed the Fish as his acquaintances nicknamed him. He is slippery. Only he and his wife know the secret to what makes him untouchable, they are the only ones who know what offers maximum protection against any form of charges.

In his family, Taelo is a real father, he loves his two boys dearly, but 'Matau never gives him a rest on accusing him of showing more liking to Limpho than Tokelo. In his response, he said, "I both love them, only that you have a tendency of making Limpho feel inferior, I have a bound duty to care for him." Limpho is the elder son in the family. He is in fact a son of Taelo's sister who died long ago, leaving Limpho at the tender age of five. Taelo took him into his household and raised him as his own. The relationship between Limpho and Tokelo is one of grudging respect and total mistrust solely because 'Matau has instilled in Tokelo's mind that Limpho is not his real brother, he is just trying to occupy his position as eldest son.

Taelo apprecites Limpho because he is unlike his own son. While Tokelo is raucous and indifferent, Limpho is sensitive and caring. He often wishes Limpho had more of an aptitude for his businesses, however, he has shown no interest. Limpho was instead into Physics and Computer Science, completing his final year at the National University of Lesotho. It is Tokelo who proved his prowess. His skills and expertise in his father's businesses are remarkably awe-inspiring as he dedicates and devotes his time to working with his father. Due to his wife's earnest entreaties, Taelo even promised Tokelo that he is going to be the heir of his empire. Tokelo abandoned his studies in the University of Free State when he failed his second year, his father advised him to go back to school, but his mother told him otherwise, "You don't need to be a book-worm like Limpho, you must follow in your father's foot-steps." He eventually resorted to listening to his mother as she showed him far better advantages.

What Tokelo did for the business was to organise meetings between his father and business acquaintances, and in this way he was more like his father's personal assistant. It is beyond reasonable doubt that Tokelo knew how the corporate world was through the knowledge he gleaned from his father. He developed an insatiable thirst for one day becoming a respected businessman like his father.

*

After a very long pause, his wife breaks in, "Ntate what is that you want to tell us? Is it very important?" Taelo is staring into space, not uttering a word. However, he knows that the time has come in which he has to extract himself from a twisted web of lies and deception he has firmly entrenched himself into throughout his life. He has no other alternative but abide by the rules of his forefathers because no mortal being can fight fate. The legacy that had been handed down from the ancestors must continue.

He finally manages to return to his senses, he continues in a rather firm tone, his voice deep and gravelly, "As I was trying to say, I'm asking you to organize *Boipeletso,* where all my relatives will be present together with *Ntate* Mosika." Tokelo asks, "When do you want this ceremony Ntate?" "It must be tomorrow, but let me speak," Taelo responds. 'Matau complains, "Ntate Taelo, will you go straight into it, you have kept us in suspense for too long." Glancing covertly at 'Matau, Taelo goes on, "The visits I'm having from my dead grandfathers are becoming a scary nightly ritual. They are telling me that if I still disobey them this time, I'll not be forgiven."

Tokelo has never in his life seen his father this appalled. He feels as though they are caught up in a middle of some endless terrifying nightmare. He asks, "What do they want, a feast, food, cows? We promise we will do anything they want if it means you will recover from your illness." Taelo replies, "My son, they want more. The truth is I have been blessed by my ancestors with a gift, a gift that no one in this world can take away from me."

It is the gift of medicine Taelo is talking about. The indestructible gift that is meant to be passed from generation to generation for all eternity. He has to pass it onto the next generation for his soul to be at liberty. It has been so through the centuries.

When 'Matau gets wind of what is happening, she interrupts him before he can finish, "Ntate do you really need to go deep into those details, they belong to the past, let us concentrate on the future and forget the past because…." She cannot finish what she was about to say. Taelo angrily interrupts her, his voice is a whiplash, "'Matau, what you now call the past is the prevailing situation that's haunting me day and night. The gods have spoken and their word is final. I'm ordered to give Limpho all my wealth and bless my own son with the gift of medicine. This is the only right way, and this is what I intend to tell everyone at the ceremony tomorrow."

Taelo further continues, "Lots of food should be prepared, Limpho today you must fetch a cow at Sehlabeng-sa-Thuathe. Find Ntate Khobotle's *mophato*, that is where I received my first initiation ritual. Tokelo, you will also travel to Morija today to get Ntate Mosika, he can't be summoned here by a phone call. Please my son, explain my situation to him, he will come. He is the only one who can help me."

By the time Taelo finishes, 'Matau is a nervous wreck. Astounded by what she is hearing, she explodes, "Limpho will you excuse us for a moment, this family needs some time alone." Hesitantly, Limpho goes out of the room. Tokelo stands bewildered,, eyes to the ground, not sure what conclusion to draw out of what his father has just said. 'Matau thunders, "Taelo, what are you saying, are you telling us that you are turning your back against your son, your own flesh, squandering everything we have worked hard for all these years to that tramp who doesn't even know who his father is? Is this the way you thank Tokelo? What happened to the promise that he's going to be your heir?"

Tokelo is overwhelmed with a great sense of despair. He does not believe that his father is not leaving him even the smallest fraction of what he thought he deserved. Taelo explains, "Matau things are no longer in my control as I'm preparing my way home. Tokelo my son, preserve and use the gift rightfully, I don't want you suffer like me."

'Matau mutters, "I can't listen to this!" as she grabs Tokelo by his clothes and drags him into the kitchen. She starts taunting him, "Tokelo what is this, why can't you stand up to your father and tell him you demand what's rightfully yours?" He replies, "M'e, I've never in my life seen my father in this state, he is so afraid, I'm in no position to argue with him, he has already said it, he has no control over what is happening now."

'Matau can hardly bring herself to believing what she is hearing. She continues letting out her frustrations on her son, "Tokelo I didn't raise you to become a coward. Fight for what's lawfully yours. How are we going to survive in this money-hungry-jungle with the so-called gift of eternity, which I am not certain is a blessing or a curse! What should sink into your thick skull is that once Limpho takes inheritance of everything, he is going to leave us here hungry, searching for his long lost father." Tokelo retorts, "What do you want me to do 'M'e, Ntate has already said it, prophecy has to be fulfilled!"

"Prophecy...prophecy...what do you know of prophecy? Listen to me Tokelo and listen very carefully, before you were even born your father got sick, very sick, and we didn't know what was wrong until he was told that he had a calling. He was destined to become a poor doctor. I wouldn't settle for that because I didn't marry a traditional doctor! I'm a Christian. I knocked some sense into him and showed him how he could use the so-called gift of eternity. No one else knows except his nosy family that he was destined to be a traditional doctor. Look today, your father is a great man, a leader. We are living in a fine house. Look at the variety of our businesses, our cars. Not a single family here in Ha-Thetsane has achieved this much."

'Matau is raging with anger, she cannot prevent herself from shouting. All this while, Limpho is standing outside the kitchen door. He hears the heated argument 'Matau is engaged in with her son. She goes on, "How do you think we have gained all this? You don't have the faintest idea, right? Now listen, I made your father a real man, I told him to protect himself. No one can touch him. They will accuse him today and tomorrow drop charges against him. My son, I know that's what you have always wanted, are you going to let Limpho take everything that's rightfully yours?"

Tokelo can hardly conceal his surprise, "You know what 'M'e, today I've seen the other side of you. Now I wonder if you even love him. But it's obvious. I was not ready for this idea of the gift of medicine, but to show you that you can't push me around, I'll have to live with it. Unlike you, I love my father, and that is why I'll do whatever it takes to help him. The ceremony is still on tomorrow, I'm leaving in the afternoon to get Ntate Mosika!" Tokelo storms out of the room leaving alone.

'Matau stands startled, not knowing her next move. The only person she is counting on is turning his back against her. She grits her teeth and feels like breaking something, "Someday you will thank me my child! You can't understand a thing right now, this is a real world where one needs to survive. If you won't do anything, I know my role, a woman holds the knife by the sharp edge. I'll do everything in my power to see to it that all these absurd assumptions stop, I swear, there won't be a ceremony here tomorrow, and that scary old savage they call Mosika won't lay his foot here, the dead would rise from their graves!"

The mere mention of the name Mosika sends blood-curdling terror through 'Matau. Throughout their entire marriage, she pleaded with her husband not to mention that name in their household. 'Matau despises him because he never forgets anything. He narrates events that occurred many years back as though they happened yesterday without leaving details. It is Mosika who trained Taelo into being *mochonoko,* one who is trained to be a traditional healer. He is the one who further initiated Taelo into becoming *ngaka*, a traditional healer. 'Matau knows Taelo has a firm belief that Mosika is the only person who could successfully communicate with the ancestors on his behalf.

The great Mosika is known for being able to speak the language of the spirits as he goes into a trance and travels the lands of the ancestors. Some say he killed a python at the age of 6, while some say he could strike with lightning. Others maintain that he has the power to command the celestial waters from the heavens while others have a belief that he is enlightened by *Mmopi*, the creator, as he knows the truths of the past and the future. *Mosika Batho,* the guardian of people, as his clansmen refer to him, went through and completed 7 dreadful rituals of initiation.

All of his initiations took place in different parts of Africa as he lived amongst many tribes, some of which include the Maasai tribe of Kenya, Bahurutsi tribe of Western Zambia and the Akan tribe of

Ghana. He was first initiated in Mashonaland and leant the secrets of the Matobo Mountains. As a custodian of sacred knowledge, he is the knower of the ancient secrets of these many tribes. He speaks the tongues of many clans as one language. The great Mosika Batho, who sings songs of the ancient ones, *Bakalanga,* people of the sun. He dances in animalistic gestures of the *Bathoa,* those that evoke the mighty spirits. He knowledgeable in the cosmological philosophy of the Igbo.

The atmosphere in the house is grim. A wave of sadness has swept over Taelo's family. What he told his family turned out to be a spark which transformed into raging flames of fire, destroying his family to utter despair. Everything looks grey and bleak. What occurs to 'Matau as a pressing legitimate question is - how she is going to survive once Limpho has wiped out her own assets? She tells herself that she will do whatever it takes to prevent Taelo from announcing to other family members that he is leaving Limpho with the wealth she has worked hard for.

In the evening, Taelo's sons embark on their respective journeys as their father ordered, leaving 'Matau and Taelo home. Tokelo drives to Morija while Limpho catches a taxi to Sehlabeng-sa-Thuathe. After reaching Mosika Batho's homestead, Tokelo does as he was told, though is quite surprised as it seems Mosika Batho was already expecting him. When giving the account of his father's sickness, Tokelo worries as it appears to him as though Mosika Batho is not eager to listen. Tokelo is informed that they will leave the next morning back to Taelo's place. He has to spend a night at Mosika Batho's home. That night, he hardly sleeps. The whole night, he can hear the old man mumbling phrases he barely understands.

Similarly, Limpho's journey is successful as he finds Khobotle's place and is given the cow his father had asked for. Khobotle tells him that he has to travel the entire night with the cow so that he arrives at Ha-Thetsane before dawn. Khobotle orders his youngest son, Tlotliso to go together with Limpho as he might find it challenging to travel at night in the woods with a cow. They both set out on a journey, Limpho timidly expressing his fears for traveling in the dark night without a car. "The moon is bright. It tells us that it's going to be a safe night," Tlotliso assures him. When Limpho regains his composure, he mentions that he has brought torches that can be used to provide light. However, Tlotliso advises him otherwise, "That kind of light will distract the cow."

The night is calm as Tlotliso has promised although Limpho continues to air his discomforts, "It looks like it's going to rain, and we will be home when it does hopefully." On the other hand, Tlotliso takes pleasure in easing Limpho's worries by explaining that when stars are clearly visible in the sky, the chances of rainfall are scarce. He further tells him to learn to study the night sky, as every time he will see wonders. "It's only one star called *Tosa* that is not shining bright tonight, maybe it's gone to rest." Limpho is baffled by the relevance of the matter. He responds, "To clearly know why it's not bright, we will need instruments to see far away things. Tlotliso argues, "No, we don't need instruments at all, *Mmopi* has put all things out there for us to see with our eyes."

In order to refute Tlotliso, Limpho feels he has to substantiate his argument by being academic. He goes on explaining to Tlotliso how some elements in nature cannot be seen with naked eyes. Giving him an example of an atomic structure in very simple terms, describing how an atom, nucleus and electrons cannot be seen with eyes, but instruments. He describes that when an instrument like a microscope is used, the atomic structure is clearly seen. His analysis is detailed, yet comprehensible to a lay person like his companion. "At the centre, there is a nucleus while the electrons are found around the nucleus," narrates Limpho. However Tlotliso disagrees, "All those things you mentioned can be seen. You talk of your atom, I see the universe, you talk of your nucleus I see the sun, you talk of those electrons, I see these stars and this earth."

Limpho is perplexed. He is not sure how to further disprove his companion and he inwardly admits that his companion is right. From the illustration that has been shared by Tlotliso, he is able to make sense of the abstract knowledge cloaked in mystery he has been taught at school. He fully understands that an atom is the solar system. At the centre of an atom there is the nucleus. In the same way, within the solar system there is the sun. Around the nucleus, the electrons move, while in the same way the planets move around the sun. As a scholar, he realizes that the only thing that differs is the size - the movements and revolutions are the same, and the laws of magnetic attraction are the same.

It becomes clear to him that his companion's understanding of the world is beyond ordinary. Tlotliso has reduced his abstract understanding of physics to common concrete knowledge. In as much as he thought they had different viewpoints earlier, Limpho is amazed to see how similar they are.

He feels imbued with love for Tlotliso's natural way of life. He is woken up from his reverie as Tlotliso states that *Mphatlalatsane*, the morning star, will soon rise. Limpho asks, "So how do I acquire this knowledge you have?" Tlotliso laughs modestly and further explains that it is *kooma*, the secret of men who have gone to the mountain for proper initiation rituals.

From a far distance, Limpho can see fire burning at his father's compound. Through this, he is assured that they will arrive just in time, before all the preparations for the ceremony can take place. They are welcomed by an old man dressed in regal wear, holding a bucket and *lechoba*, the tail of a cow. He silently starts splashing water on them with his *lechoba*, goes to the cow, splashes it with water and recites some chants. He finally breaks out, "Sons, go inside, we have been waiting for you. This cow must be slaughtered now before sunrise. It is going to accompany your father, go inside the house. Your family is waiting for you." A cloud of confusion surrounds Limpho, he is not sure of what conclusion to draw from what he is hearing. Tlotliso tries to calm him down, "*Tosa,* the brightest star in the night sky was dim, don't despair, its death brings rebirth."

When entering the house, Limpho is confronted by hysteric moans of 'Matau. He finally makes sense of what the old man outside told him. Tokelo tells him that he arrived at around four in the morning with Mosika Batho finding Taelo dead. With a tear-washed face, Tokelo explains Limpho him that 'Matau says their father suffered a heart attack at night, but Mosika Batho has made vague statements suggesting that 'Matau has something to do with their father's death. He further tells Limpho that Mosika says Taelo's burial should be on the very same day and should be a nocturnal performance for the ancestors.

'Matau argues that it is impossible to bury her husband on the day of his death because she has to make insurance claims first. She says the burial can only happen after a week. Limpho is informed by Tokelo that he, Limpho, is the one who has to make a final decision as their father has written everything under his name. Limpho's face immediately becomes pale and he feels as though his whole world has been shattered instantaneously. With a very bitter heart, he tells Tokelo that it will be best to make the decision with their relatives who were already coming for *Boipeletso* ceremony.

139

By around nine in the morning, Taelo's relatives are flocking in. To their dismay, they find their brother dead. Tokelo briefs them about Taelo's intentions in asking for the ceremony of *Boipeletso*, "Words can't express the horror I feel. My father's life has been cut short on the very same day that he wanted to ask for forgiveness from all of us. He wanted to ask for forgiveness from our ancestors for abandoning them and he told us that the ancestors will only be appeased if I accept the gift of medicine. He has left everything in Limpho's control. He had asked Ntate Mosika Batho to perform his cleansing ceremony. Ntate Mosika states that my father's spirit can still be cleansed only if he is buried tonight, but my mother says he should be buried next week. In saying these, I'm asking for the opinions of my elders in this matter. I'm also asking Ntate Mosika to explain in detail the manner in which he says my father's funeral should be conducted."

There are murmurs of disbelief in the room. Mosika stands up from where he is seated to address them. A cold silence fills the entire room, it is broken by an ancestral chant recited by a creaky voice of Mosika Batho, "*Ramaseli Rammoloki Tlatlamacholo, khant'setsa leseli la hao ho Bakoena ba Maieane oa khomo, mora Motloheloa, ba 'Mamotetenene oa khosi, ba khatampi e ntle, sebapalla, ba maleruo le tloha ho khomo le ee ho motho!*" He continues in a heavy voice filled with pure venom, "They will be condemned by ancestral gods, they will become wanderers, and their sanity will be slashed bluntly for trying to stand in the way of gods." From where she is seated 'Matau gives an audible sigh.

Mosika goes on, "A grave will be dug today for him to begin his journey this night to the ancestors. His body will be wound up in an ox skin. It will be bound in ropes made of grass. He will be placed in the grave in a sitting position facing east. A few seeds of pumpkin, sorghum and maize will be thrown beside the body and his grave will be covered by soil. This way, the ancestors will gracefully accept this spirit." After this, he slowly walks out of the room leaving everyone transported in a completely different realm. In this moment, Tokelo tells his elders that he is accepting the will of the ancestors. He will follow the infinite spiritual gift and undergo training to become *ngaka*. The family engages in a discussion about the nature of Taelo's burial, the entire case hinged on honoring his wish of seeking purification. They finally come to the shared decision of going Mosika Batho's way.

'Matau's frustration boils over. She dashes out of the room and heads to her bedroom. Talks of the burial that is bound to happen tonight continue. Once the plan is formulated Limpho declares that after his father's burial, he is joining Tlotliso at *Ntate* Khobotle's initiation school. This news leaves everyone scandalized.

Meanwhile, Tokelo is struggling to come to terms with the fact that his father is really gone. When the reality of the matter gradually dawns upon him he plunges into a deep sorrow. He restlessly questions the possibility that his father's death was premature. He is disturbed from his thoughts by his mother who enters the room dressed shabbily in a cape that she wears on Sundays. She shouts at the top of her voice, "Traitors, witches, evil spirits, I cast you out. This is my house. Everyone, go! Limpho you won't get anything, everything is mine. Everyone out! Leave those cups and spoons, they are mine!" It becomes clear to Tokelo that 'Matau is spinning out of control, he moves to restrain her but Mosika Batho stops him, "Those the gods seek to destroy, they first drive crazy, let her be, the price needs to be paid."

Our Little Mystery

Rethabile Manong

In a frenzy, the first high school school term started. Boys and girls Keketso's age were regularly seen whining or trotting happily behind their mothers'skirts in town for back-to school shopping sprees. Like a packaged bride, Keketso had found his school uniform and shoes he had had his eyes on for ages arranged in his rondavel which served as his study, sleeping quarters and bathroom. He had excitedly fitted his whole uniform on and ran outside to examine his reflection in the window for they had no floor-length mirror. What he saw in the window cast a big smile on his face, big enough to have brightened even the darkest of days.

Having delayed at his Granny's, Keketso had trouble registering for school and it was some two weeks before he enrolled into a classroom. He was assigned a desk two rows from the front and that made him very uneasy. Had it not been for the girl he shared the desk with, he would have asked for a move. Two weeks of absence had caused more harm than he had hoped. His old friends had made new friends and he had trouble fitting in. It was as if everything was a few paces ahead while he was lagging far behind. However something unexpected happaned, and it caught him off guard.

It had been an ordinary school day like any other. During lunch break, when everybody poured out excitedly, he decided to join them on their way to the school's cafeteria. He bought himself four fatcakes and a very thick slice of French polony, coupled with a tumbler of ginger-beer. He went to the back steps of the cafeteria and relished his meal. Daydreaming, he found himself laughing out at a joke he heard from his cousins a month or so ago. He quickly clasped his hand over his mouth, afraid that somebody might hear him and take him for mentally disturbed.

It wasn't long afterwards when a bell summoning them back to class rang. He quickly got up and hurried off to class. How he dreaded the girl he shared his desk with! Many a time she had cast side glances at him, regarding him in a way he never understood. How ugly her smile was! She was not the type one could even ask out, thought Keketso, squeezing into their desk. Two, five and ten minutes passed, but the teacher failed to show up.

By now the class was berserk with noise, pupils abandoned their seats and visited their "neighbours." A bevy of girls near the corner were busy applying brightly coloured nail polish and silly giggles erupted now and then. Keketso's so-called "desk-mate" also dashed off to her friends for some "hot gossip" as fondly described by that group of terrible gossip-mongers. Realising his vulnerability for failure to join in the class escapades, Keketso sought solace in his books. He had just lifted a book from its neat stack when a piece of paper slid to the floor. He picked it up and hurriedly read its astonishing contents. With an ashen face, he scanned his classmates to see if any might have accidentally slipped such a note, but all of them were deeply engrossed with some sort of clamorous misdemeanor. He re-read it and folded it and put it in his schoolbag. Like a whirlwind, it had created a terrible turmoil in his mind. Was that addressed to him? From whom? he wondered.

Dating and romantic attachments were things way over his head, so whoever summoned enough courage to ask him out was most definitely wasting her time. He once heard his cousins (who were a bit older than him) fuss about proper words to utter when asking a girl out, how worried they had seemed! Stupid, because a girl according to him was just like any other human being, addressed anyhow. How elated his cousins became when one of them related an instance when a girl asked him out and he denied. They booed him and told him they would have accepted without hesitation, for she would have saved them the trouble of thinking complex approaches to asking girls out and the embarassment felt when a girl turned them down.

Keketso sat there with his musings. He was just about to open his book when a teacher stepped into the classroom for the following period. He hardly concentrated while tricky Maths problems were being worked on. All the time, his mind kept taking him on a roller-coaster trip to the mysterious note. When the bell ending school day rang, he asked his "deskmate," who openly denied knowledge of the note and its "deliverer." He went home in a very gloomy mood, dragging his feet behing him lazily. Arriving home, he quickly changed and away he went to herd his family's little flock of goats and sheep.

A few days later when he thought the storm of confused emotions was clearing, another note showed up in his desk as mysteriously as the first one. Reluctantly, he pored over its contents. Alas! It contained the same message as the first. The second read as follows:

Dear Joy of My Heart,

I wish I were a teddy bear on your bed, so that everytime you cuddled it, you cuddle me instead. O gorgeous! You have such a lovely smile, warm enough to heat up the coldest of days! Hao, why are you doing this to me? Can't you see I love you with all my being?

XOXO

Astounded and dumbfound at the same time, he racked his brain as to what step to take next. He felt guilty for his failure to respond favourably to the first note, but how could he have when he did not even know who wrote it. An icy tinge of fear gripped him; the fear of the unknown. At last, he made his mind up, wrote a reply to the note and left it in the desk where he had found the other notes. When he came back from break, the reply note was gone, phew!

You just cannot believe the apprehension Keketso felt. He could not wait for the notes to show up agian. Two days came and went swiftly by, still no sign of the notes. He was at this juncture afraid that maybe his reply had been very harsh. He was naive and blamed that on himself. "How I wish I had listened to my cousins when they were giving me free tutorials on these matters," he bitterly reflected.

His keeness in searching his desk every morning, break and lunch seemed to have grown overnight. He slept, ate and studied little, for his mind was continously reeling with expectations from his mysterious correspondent. One afternoon, when his last rays of hope were slowly dwindling, he found what he had been longing for. His heart made many attempts to jump out of his chest, but he did not care. The burden he had been carrying lifted instantly.

"Meet me behind the Woodwork Block during free-period" read the note. Time dragged slower than ever. At last the bell rang for free-period and he lingered intentionally in the class so he could spot the person who would go towards the Woodwork Block. He was surprised when none walked in that direction. Cautiously he made his way to his mysterious destination. Thanks to the Botanical Project at school, there was a, lush green lawn near the Woodwork block, flanked by numerous flower-beds, sandstone bird-baths and benches lined along peach trees. The place was indeed a paradise. How fresh the air combing the peach trees felt on his cheeks!

Having scanned the benches for some time, voila! There she was, sitting on the bench farthest from the rest, her head slightly bent forward into the open book on her lap. She looked graceful with her rich, brown hair showering her shoulders. Keketso felt weak at the knees, however he pressed forward. At the sound of a breaking twig Keketso had stepped on, she turned towards him. "Hi," she said, standing up in a welcoming gesture. Keketso faltered for a while. "Er... hello," he managed to say. As they both sat down, she produced a box of chocolate and offered Keketso some. His mind was miles away, for his worst fears were confirmed. She was an Indian girl he had seen once or twice at school. "Oh God, how I wish I had said something nice to her greeting," he silently observed.

He almost wished he had not come. He was caught between the Devil and deep sea, wondering how everybody would react to their relationship, especially their families. "Keketso," the girl roused him from his reverie. "I can't believe I've finally found you, boy! You are such a catch." Keketso smiled at her anxiously. "I'm flattered and fortunate to have a girl as beautiful as you," he replied nervously.

You know how conversations of lovebirds fare, don't you? She turned out to be Sarah, the daughter of one of the wealthiest Indian businessmen in the whole country. Though Indian, she was born in Lesotho, and spoke fluent Sesotho. How sweet and calming her voice was to Keketos's taut muscles. They exchanged cellphone numbers and agreed to meet again. Keketso asked about the mysterious notes, to which Sarah responded by telling him they got to him through his "deskmate" who was good friends with Sarah. Relief swept over Keketso like the kiss of a virgin morning.

Several weeks later, Sarah invited Keketso to see where she stayed. Her rented, single room was welcomingly warm and cosy. Her three-quarter bed leaned against the wall behind the door. It was covered with a lovely duvet of the purest pink colour, with two, big, fluffy continental pillows forming a headboard of some sort. A neat row of scatter cushions followed, on which teddy bears, stuffed bunnies and

146

ponies nestled. They resembled a crowded animal home, if only they made sounds. Keketso drank it all in not missing even a single item. Keketso and Sarah had stolen out of the school campus when the sports participants took to the grounds. They had grown quite close since their first rondezvous, so much that Keketso could not stand a day without seeing her. However, fright dwelt in his heart whenever he was with Sarah. His heart would give two beats instead of one.

Now, in her room, they reclined on the bed in an affectonate emrace. Keketso thought Sarah must be hearing the wild beating of his heart.

"Baby relax. Why are you so tense?" Sarah said, fixing her gaze on Keketso's sweaty face. "I don't bite hey." Keketso disentangled from the embrace, took both Sarah's hands and looked her straight in the eyes. Dancing in them was a mixture of pleasure, amusement and worry. "It's just that...that...that everytime I'm this close to you, my heart grows wings, " Keketso said, heaving a long sigh. "I mean... you make me feel like I'm floating on cloud nine." The corners of Sarah's mouth crinkling sweetly, she gave him a smile that made all his fears evaporate. "Oh, come here. I love you," she said, whispering. As Kekstso's slightly parted lips quivered with expectation she kissed him nice and full. Keketso's head felt like it would explode with tinklings from Sarah's kiss. She then laid her thickly-carpeted head on his chest and Keketso couldn't help but stroke it gently. The afternoon lazed on and the two lovebirds talked, laughed, teased each other, joked and did things.

For weeks and months to follow, sweet love notes kept pouring into Keketso's desk though they were not mysterious anymore. He responded tenderly to them all, some imprinted with Sarah's heavily-lipsticked lips. School life became enjoyable, though at times he would be annoyed by Sarah, who never wanted to part with him. She liked to be collected from her flat to school everyday and to be taken back after school. This was tiring, but he had no option but to do it. Sometimes Sarah would be easily irritated by minor things and throw big tantrums. This new behaviuor startled Keketso out of his wits.

One day, his classmate approached him and they talked at length. He addressed Keketso's relationship with Sarah. "My brother, I'm worried about you," concern visible on his face. Keketso's smile faded and his face clouded over instantly. "What are you talking about? Huh?" Keketso asked angrily. The classmate felt like backing off, but he braced himself. "I know I shouldn't be saying this, but the brotherly love I have for you binds me to. Be aware of Sarah. That girl will bring nothing but harm to you. She will suck you bone-dry and leave you for greener pastures. Haven't you noticed how round she is these days? Watch out my bro." Keketso's already clenched fists were ready to fly but something held him back. He looked long on his classmate, and his fists drooped with shame, he turned his back on him. His classmate's words had borne into him than he had bargained for.

It was about mid-May when another note turned up. June examinations were around the corner and Keketso was taking to preparation seriuosly, so he shoved it away deciding to read it later.

Love

'Let's talk tonight, usual place, usual time,' read the short note. It turned out, Sarah was six months pregnant. Keketso wished the earth could open up and swallow him whole. His biggest fear was how to tell his parents. For weeks, he worked out plans to terminate Sarah's pregnancy, but evertually fought against such an idea. An innocent, unborn baby deserves love, he would reason. He, himself, was a child too, how could he father another child? He didn't know.

The news of the pregnancy finally got out and led to heated meetings between the two families. Keketso's self-esteem took a knock for the sadness he had caused his parents. He felt he was left with no choice but to make Sarah his wife. "A Sesotho saying states that a woman is a devil's match," his mother said one evening. "My son, I promise to stand by you no matter what. I'm also proud of you for the right decison you have made of offering to marry that girl. I admire your courage despite your father and uncles' disapproval, and for that, I forgive you wholeheartedly." Keketso stood transfixed before his mother, tears cascading down his cheeks. His mother stretched her big arms out for a comforting motherly embrace. Keketso vowed in his heart that he would be a better son to his parents and husband to his future wife. However, his sixth sense told him that even though he agreed to marry Sarah, something strange had happaned between them, he just couldn't prove what it was. He decided to give it time, sure that one day he would get to the bottom of it, even if it meant moving heaven and earth.

For days, Keketso nursed his thoughts as a tongue would a sore tooth. The more he thought about it, the harder it became to crack. He thought of secretly consulting a local sangoma, but gave up the idea. "Sangomas, all they do is launder your money," he had once heard his mother say. "Instead of fortune-telling as they claim, they spread evil animosities even among brothers," she had said, spitting disgustedly to the ground. Taking up the tone of a sangoma in a trance, she imitated, "Hayi, hayi, makhosi, makhosi! Watch out, watch out! U jeoa ke nta tsa kob'a hao! Vumani boo!" Keketso couldn't help, but smile to such a distant memory. Had his mother been auditioning, she could have made it to Broadway.

One blistering cold afternoon in June found Keketso on his way back from his usual visit to his fiancé. Having left home early that day, he had forgotten to put on a jacket, for it had seemed warm. How

149

decietful Lesotho's weather could be in winter! After a few hours at Sarah's, the sky had turned wintry, and thin, lonely clouds had scuddled quickly by in the fury of the, wind which had arrived unexpectedly. People hurried to the warmth of their hissing paraffin heaters and eye-stinging, smokey fires. Unaware of the time, it was quite late when Keketso stepped outside Sarah's home and the cold that greeted him warned that he would freeze to death even before he reached his residence; several kilometres away.

He borrowed Sarah's jacket and beanie and gave her a goodbye kiss. Then he firmly adjusted the beanie closer to his ears, zipped up the jacket and raced homeward. The wind howled violently in his face. The sound it made was like somebody whispering consipratorially into his ears. It quickly became dark, for the afterglow of the sun in winter barely lasts. He had covered most of the distance home when his hand felt something in the jacket pocket. Pulling it out, he realised it was a reciept from a chemist he did not know. However, he could not make out what was the purchase in the already feeble light. He decided to look at it when he got home.

There were no fires flickering in the open hearths, no delighted voices of children playing and no moon when he reached his neighborhood. Only dogs barked at his heels in the inky darkness. His parents had already gone to bed, so he went straight to his sleeping quarters. There, he found his dinner perfectly arranged on the table by his mother, a common practice when he had had a late night. After warming his hands on the paraffin heater, he decided to check out the reciept. As he read it,his body went numb, cold and hot at the same time. He couldn't believe his eyes. His appetite vanished instantly and he climbed into bed fully clothed. The next morning, his mother found the dinner untouched and the bed empty. She thought her son did not turn up the previous night. By then, Keketso was sitting in Sarah's bedroom, his tear-stained face twisted and sad. Sarah's face also mirrored Keketso's. They sat facing away from each other.

"Keketso, you are a good, decent gentleman and you do not deserve this," Sarah broke the silence, half speaking, half whispering amidst tears. "I had to do it this way. I was already three months pregnant when I first met you in February. I bought the pregnancy test kit in December as you can see the date on that reciept. Things leading to my pregnancy were ugly, really ugly. So, when I saw you, I picked you out as my only saviour, I am sorry." She put her face in her hands and wailed bitterly. Overcome by pity, Keketso took her in his arms and rocked her back and forth comfortingly.

Minutes passed, and at last both regained their composures. "Sweetheart, do you mind telling what happaned?" Keketso softly enquired. "Not until I have washed my face, freshened up and have fixed us breakfast. Lets talk over a fresh cup of coffee," Sarah replied. Keketso nodded and with that Sarah rose to her feet and went towards the bathroom. She shouted over her shoulder, "I wont be long," and Keketso looked at her longingly. At the breakfast table, Keketso bit hungrily at the tender, fried chunks of juicy bacon and washed them down with sweet, creamy coffee. Meanwhile, Sarah began her story:

"Last winter, dad had come home dejected and sad. His tender had been rejected by the Board of Directors of Sekoti-Mpate Mall, that new mall that has recently opened in Lifotholeng. You know the place, right?"

Keketso just nodded for his mouth was full to speak.

"That was to be the highlight of dad's career as a businessman, so when his tender met the rejection, all his dreams and ambitions came tumbling down. However, he did not easily give up like a coward, so he approached one member of the Board of Directors and pledged to do anything to save his business reputation. At such a proposal, that board member realised that he had an opportunity, so he asked father for my hand in marriage. That upset my father a great deal, but he decided to give it a try. I only learned the news when a few days later, mom and him approached me and told me that this marriage was the only way to save our family business. I openly denied it, reasoning that I didn't want a 'packaged' groom, but should instead be given a chance to choose one myself, one that will suit me."

Many arguments sprang up for weeks until my mom took my side. She pleaded with my father, but to no avail. Seeing my father was not going to compromise on the cruel bargain my left home. Things got really bad after she departed. You can just imagine the turmoil I was in. I was truly torn between two fighting forces; mom and dad. After mom left, I lived like a prisoner in my dad's home. Then one day, dad came home in a jovial mood after months of hostility towards me. He announced that we were invited to dinner. For the first time in months, I went out shopping and did my hair and nails. Our host was the very board member I have just told you about. After introductions and dinner, he took me on a tour of his grand house. He told me his wife had died in a car accident two years earlier so he was looking for a new wife. To him and my father I would only make a perfect substitute for his late wife. How disgusting! We were went deeper and deeper into hismansion and in an instant, he forced himself onto me. What took place afterwards I do not know for I was numb with rage at dad and this stranger."

Now that I am pregnant with his child, dad told me I was attached to this man, no matter what. Dad's business is now flourishing at that mall, but at the expense of my happiness and virginity. Well, I have forgiven him because that's what any father and husband could have done for his family. Mom nearly went mad when she heard what had befallen me. That has ruined chances of her getting back together with dad. So, I saw you and forged this plan in my mind in an attempt to extricate myself from all this. Now, my cover has been blown and I have to face this bitter reality from a different perspective. I am sorry Keketso, I didn't mean to hurt you, I'm terribly sorry," she said tears stealing down her cheeks in torrents.

Keketso could not bear it any longer, so he abandoned his breakfast and hugged her. "It's ok my love. You are not alone, we're in this together. We will work this out, I promise," he said reassuringly. Just then he felt a movement in Sarah's already bulging belly. "Ah!" he exclaimed excitedly moving his hand tenderly up and down the bulge. "Our little mystery can't wait to meet us." They both laughed.

Nonyana tsa siba leng li fofa mmoho

'Mant'sabeng Lifalakane Tuoane

Mosotho o ne a opile khomo lenaka ha a re nonyana tsa tšiba-ngoe li fofa 'moho le hore ngoan'a lekhala o tsamaea ka lekeke joalo ka 'm'ae. Motsaneng o bitsoang Ha Koali, teropong ea Teya-teyaneng, ho ne ho'na le bashanyana ba babeli, mabitso a bona e le Mohlolo le Ralihotetso.

Mohlolo o ne a le meeka, a hlaha ka lintho tse makatsang ka mehla eohle. Hase feela, hee o ne a tsoa mothong hle. Ntat'ae e ne e le lekako la monna; meketeng le lipitsong ho ne ho utluoa ka eena, e le eena seea-le-moea. Mafung teng o ne a ipha seabo sa ho buella Morena le Mokhethoa ha ba le sieo. Ho tla u makatsa ke hore motho oa teng e ne e le moipehi. O ne a se leqe ho bolela ka mokhoa oo e neng e le motho oa maemo ea ikhonang a neng a sa a khathalle ho tšeptjoa. Ha a ne a ka apara kobo ea hae ea letairi e 'mala oa lengau, a e akhela lehetleng la letsoho le letšehali, a kena tseleng, Ao! E ne eba li raohile.

Mohlang Mohlolo a hlahang ntata'e o ne a ema thajaneng ea motse a tlola-tlola, a kuputsa maroele, a khethetsa makoeba, a ithoka a re:

Hona ke mohlolo-hlolo 'fela sa Ba-roma
Phoka ea lala motšeare tsatsi le chabile
Ea lala basali ba etsoa merapelong
Ba tsoa rapella khotso le pula ka har'a naha ea Motlotlehi
Mohlaope e re tlisetsa nala le khora Phoka
Bonang mohlolo, chaba se maketse
Re makaletse ho bona ngoan'e motona
Pholo ea letlaka kabeloa-manong

154

Pholo ea letlaka katisa-leloko
Ka eena motse o eketsehile
Basali tsohang le hlabe melilietsane!
Tsanyaolang hobane kajeno le tsoaletsoe mokhoenyana
Ke eona Phoka ea habo 'Malisebo le Teketsi
Ea khaola ea ea!

Ha e le Ralihotetso eena e ne e le ho mahlo a *lephekhe* tjena, molancheche o sa li halikelang ho li ja. E ne e le phepheletsane eo hangata ha litaba li hlahile, li neng li tšoanela ba bang ntle le eena. Ka bomalimabe e ne e se e le khutsana-khulu, a iphelela ba linonyana. Bahlankana ba babeli bana ba ne ba ntšana se inong, e ne e ka mafihlelana-khotla.

Ka 2007, Mohlolo le Ralihotetso ba ne ba etsa sehlopha sa bone (Form D). Bobeli bona bo ne bo sena thahasello lithutong tsa bona hohang, lihlooho tsa bona li ne tšetse boea feela. Mosebetsi oa bona e ne e le ho sitisa le ho luba baithuti ba bang. Tsietsi ea Ralihotetso e kholo ka ho fitisisa ke hore e ne e le raborokoana. Ha a ne a ka inama feela ha tichere e ntse e ruta e ne e ba o ile le maili-ili, ke ka hoo a neng a iphathahanya ka ho tšoenya baithuti bang ebe o ba betsa ka liphephechana. Moithuti ea neng a lula pela hae eena o ne a felile ke lifeisi tsa mehla hobane Ralihotetso o ne a lula a mo qosetsa hore na o ne a sa a mo tsose ke'ng. Lebaka la tlhekefetso e kana-kana ke hore hore Ralihotetso ha a ne a khalehile, o ne a baka litšeho tse sa feleng, motho oa teng o ne a a ahlama ha a khalehile, hoo ntsintsi e ne e ka kena eaba ea tsoa. Liqhenqhe li ne li lula li leketlile, a bile a pasela ka ho sheba ka leihlo le le leng ebe letsoho le letona le tšetlehile lerameng. Joale e be ho sa tla khona ho ho tona!

Sehloho sa hae e ne e le sa hore ha bookameli ba sekolo ba 'motsa hore na hobaneng a ne a hlekefetsa bana ba bang o ne a ikarabella ka hore toro ea hae ke hoba lesole ha a hola!

*

Ka letsatsi le leng e ne e re ha Mohlolo a fihla sekolong hoseng a fumane buka ea hae eo a neng a lokela ho tšoauoa ho eona e nyametse. O ne a leke ho e batla hohle eaba ha ho nko ho tsoa lemina. Eitse hang ha motsoalle oa hae a kena monyako, Mohlolo a hla mo tšela ka tsona eaba Ralihotetso a tsoelapele ho hoelehetsa ka sehlopheng a re: "Hee! *chitja,*"

Ha baithuti ba bang ba qhamisa litsebe ho utloa hore na o hoelehetsa ka le re'ng eng, a boetse a pheta ka lentsoe le bohale: "Hee chitja!"

Eare baithuti ba sa maketse, Ralihotetso a b'a sa qotsitse motho oa hae joaloka nonyana e fefoloa ke setsokotsane. Motho a re ka re oa ithotlolla, Ralihotetso ke ha a mo tšoara ka matla a bile a rara mothapo phatleng.

"Ntša buka eane eo o e nkileng, rea tseba ke oena lesholu ka mona": ke Ralihotsetso eo.

"Buka efe?" moithuti a araba ka makalo.

Eaka a ka be a se cho joalo, sehlopha kaofela ke ha se mo bokanela eaba bohle ba ntse ba re feela:"*Chitja, chitja, chitjang* ntja ena banna"!

Bomalimabe ke hore ba bang ba bona ba ne ba sa tsebe le hore na chitja eo moelelo oa eona ke ofeng. Ho sa le joalo Ralihotetso, ke eo a loma moithuti eo liraong.. Ba bang ba latela eaba ba emella ngoana eo oa batho ka meno, ba sa natse le ho puta hoa bosulu ha ba ntse ba mo loma. Ba tsoetse pele joalo ba ntse ba mo loma ho fihlela a namoleloa ke tšepe ea sekolo e ba tsebisang hore ke nako ea ho ea thapelong. Mothating ono borikhoe ba moithuti eno ba sekolo bo ne bo le marantha ka morao, a bile a lahlehetsoe ke pene ea hae ka har'a moferefereng.

Ka mor'a thapelo moithuti eo o ile a tlaleha Ralihotetso le bo mphato oa hae ho matichere. Kahlolo e ile eaba hore baetsi ba ketso eo ba rekele moithuti eo borikhoe le pene tse ncha.

Mohlolo ke ha a bua ka boikhomoso bohle a bolela hore o tla patala borikhoe pele beke e fela. the ha e le pene eona eaba o mo fa eona eane e neng e nyametse har'a morusu hobane e ne e utsuoe ke eena. 'Mali a ka ipotsa hore na ha ntat'a Mohlolo ha a ne a ntse a potoloha motse, a oroha joaloka khoho, chelete ea ho reka borikhoe eona o ne a tla e nka kae?

Ralihotetso eena kaha e ne e le molotsana, o ne a liile marama eaba o tlaleha kamoo ba chitjang ho thibela bosholu sehlopheng sa bona. Ka mor'a hore ba shebisise 'taba tsa Ralihotetso , matichere a ile a li chaella monoana ka lebaka la hore le bona ba ne ba tšoenyehile ke bosholu ba libuka sekolong seo. Baithuti ba lihlopha tse ling ba ile ea nyarosa ke litaba tseo hoo ba neng ba se ba sa kene sehlopheng sa bo Ralihotetso. Ho feta moo, Ralihotetso le Mohlolo ke ha ba qapa leano la hore banana bona ha ba tla *chitjuoe* ka ho akoa ke bashanyana ba sehlopha seo kaofela ho fihlela ba khathala.

Summer Blues

Tebby Letsie Schoeman

And then everybody wants summer to arrive and be singing "Ke December Boss." But exactly how many sing the summer song to the very end? Love, as with life, is like grass; it springs, blossoms, withers and dies. The sad truth is, not everybody's grass is evergreen.

SUMMER

Today is not exactly one of my best days, but I cannot show a sad face to the commoners. I'm gonna wear the usual mask I so skillfully wear when times are this shitty. But what was I thinking? How could have I been so stupid?

This morning I sat in front of the mirror for almost two hours trying to conceal the scars left by disappointment and dismay on my face. I must have used half the jar of mousse. When I tried pulling a cultured smile, instead of noticing the expression, I realised not even a single line was showing on my face, and I instantly felt the weight of the mask I was wearing. How shameless could that be? Who wants to wear such heavy make-up on a Friday? I ran some hot water and started scrubbing my face. I scrubbed until my skin felt hot and started turning red. I then went through the whole process of toning and moisturising, but I was more careful, more gentle this time.

But what exactly had happened to me? Who was this remorseless being trapped in my body? Where did I get all these tears? Today I almost cried when sister boss asked me how could I be one hour late on a Friday. The usual me would have just dismissed her, I always get away with almost anything, I am that cunning. But this soft, soft being inside me scares the bowels out of me, and to think the woman was not even shouting or mad at me to any degree, but was only asking, jokingly so, 'how can one be one hour late for work on a mid-month Friday?' And there I was, tears welling up in my eyes. This needs to change, I cannot go on like this; my tears are too precious to be seen.

You know, earlier today when he asked me if I would join him for sundowners, I thought to myself, 'boy has a nerve,' but then again, I allowed him to play friends with me immediately after we broke up. A stupid move, but was I not hoping the sun would rise again at some point? Every time I hear his voice, there's some unusual warmth I feel inside me, the kind that erases 'no' from one's vocabulary.

***

Riverside Mall sits at the foot of a perfectly cut hill, with Madame Pierre café offering a great view of the river flowing immaculately south and its lush surroundings. The aroma of freshly brewing coffee will keep all your senses awake, soothing your thoughts as your eyes are arrested by the beauty of Mother Nature just across the main road. The carefully selected lounge tracks playing and the roughly cut accents of the French wanna-bes keep life interesting at this café. Sitting alone, I let my thoughts sail for a moment and get lost in the bliss surrounding me. I occasionally closed my eyes and tried to separate the smell of coffee from that of cigarettes and cigars. People live large in this town. I was probably gone for a good five minutes or perhaps more when --

"Lost in a moment or searching for creative space?" Linda, the sweetest of the waitresses at Madame Pierre asked, wearing a smile you would swear she got from God himself five seconds ago.

"Lost and searching," I said, opening my eyes wider to this wonder.

"Oh, I see you had to be here first, for a security check. Would you care for a chocolate while you wait for him? We imported some from Switzerland; it's on me," she offered.

Linda is such a sweet soul. God, I love chocolate and yes, I needed the right energy before he got there. I always arrive first to our rendezvous, usually an hour before he does. Linda thinks I am crazy, but I like watching my guy approach. It almost gives me a sense of control. He must find me settled. Linda came back with the promised Swiss chocolate, and it had scents of orange rind in it. Lovely. The dark creation made love to my taste buds, stripping them of their innocence, and leaving my mouth with several blasts of palate orgasms. I let my mind run to places I had never been as I enjoyed the aftermath. The multiple orgasms in my mouth were busy reconstructing pleasure when a light kiss landed on my forehead.

What the freaking hell? That was nice, and very romantic, but who does he think he is? I thought. Donkey! I opened my eyes to a creature that seemed new, yet so familiar to me. Boy, this child! He smelled fresh and bold. Sweet Jesus, can't we exchange mothers now? I remember thinking.

"Meditating?" he asked, as he took his seat.

You know what this guy's voice did to me? It opened up my heart and lit a fire in there, unsealing the valves tightly closed in my sacred pits. Words escaped me; I just wanted to listen to him talk. But isn't he a liar too? I thought, and I closed my eyes again and to indulge in the moment before I could respond to him.

160

"Bloody chocolate be making love to me."

He laughed a little at that and reached for my hand. Not only were the taps open down there, but it was also raining cats and dogs. A trip to the Ladies was quite essential, but it had to be an artful escape. I needed to say a prayer too.

Botho acted like he could always mess with my emotions and get away with it. It was time I showed off the weight of the balls I carry on my chest. But who did he think he was? He was not even sure if he loved me. Why should we waste each other's time? Rather, why should I allow him to waste my time? I thought. I used to love this guy, shame. He used to make me feel things I have never felt before. He used to tell me he loved me, and that never implied he wanted to have sex with me. As a matter of fact, he had said he would never touch me until the day he married me. That would be in twelve days now, had Sheila not been back in the picture. Back in the picture! The fact that he sat there across from me like we were an item, yet we weren't, caused me malicious heartburn. I got up from my chair, cleared my throat, looked him straight in the eye and with burning passion I told him,

"Let me call you when I home."

The look on his face was priceless. He let me go without protest, without a word uttered. Bastard did not even care to walk me to my car. But would I have escaped if he did?

BOTHO

I do not know why I did what I did. Summer, my Summer, the Summer of my life, my warmth my joy; she does not deserve to be

161

hurt. She deserves a happy life, but is she going to get one with me? The truth is I love her just as I love Sheila. But there is something with Summer that kills me every day I think of her. She is the warmth that fills my heart, the joy that overflows from me. I have been with Sheila for the past two years and Summer, my Summer, is it five or six months?

I had difficulty going away from the mirror this morning. I was not happy with the shade of sadness that sat carelessly on my face. I must have toned and moisturised, about four times when my cheeks started burning and I knew something had been overdone. I stared at the mirror looking at the stranger it reflected. The sadness in his eyes could not be covered nor hidden by the perfect smile he had been tirelessly practising for the past three weeks. There was something about his eyes that looked like emptiness and darkness. You could tell something was missing, could it be something stolen, something lost or something thrown away?

I got stuck in traffic for almost thirty minutes. Is it not funny how we are always victims of our own doings but always want to glue the blame on someone else? The whole time I was stuck in traffic I was thinking of that miserable face I saw in my mirror. Bloody thing kept flashing in my mind. I thought of Summer, wondered how she was doing. She is not as strong as she acts. Right inside that thick looking skin of hers there's a fragile, loving person. She is like a crocodile, you would have to find her underbelly to really piss her off or pull her down. She is the type of woman who does not let her circumstances dictate her dream. She is fighter. She is a woman.

"Oh my God! You look terrible. Are you okay? Is Summer okay?"

Thato, our blabber-mouth receptionist got up from her chair to offer me a hug as I walked in to my office. I guess I looked like a zombie. She offered to make a pot of rooibos for me and lend an ear; very sweet, but she was not getting anything out of me. Thato has a talent of spreading news like wild fire. They say she studied journalism. Talk about a missed calling. Before I knew it, she was back with a pot of fresh tea, with cut lemon and honey, just the way I like it. She sat down and looked at me with those earnest, yet commanding eyes and said nothing.

"Thato, Summer is okay, I am okay. I just didn't sleep in time. Had a report to complete. Thank you for the tea and thank you for caring."

"Take your time, my ears are always ready to listen," she said getting up and giving me that 'you know I don't buy it' face.

It was very sad that I hadn't told anyone the truth. This was my baby though, I would take care of it. But what would people think of me if I shared the news? Thank God I had no meetings, no interaction with clients. I sat there at my desk without will or purpose, almost numb. Eventually, I figured it was time I do what I came there for – to be useful. I took my computer out of its bag and switched it on. A gush of warm blood swept through my face as the screen came to life. My heart pounded in excitement. Was sweat on my hands? She is beautiful, I thought. Summer, my Summer. She has been my screensaver from the day she and I started exchanging photos about four months ago. I do not know how it all happened. I mean, she was the first girl, the first woman to make it to my screensaver. Since then she has been the first thing I see each morning before my daily madness starts and she has been the last thing I see before going to bed. She gave the courage I needed, the motivation to wake up the next morning. She was the reason I kept going. Feeling my muscles pull my face into a genuine smile, I realized what I had been missing.

Despite the complete silence policy in the office, I took out my phone and made the call that changed my whole morning. It felt like new day altogether. I was like a baby who just let out his first cry. Free. I promised myself that I would get to Madame Pierre at least thirty minutes earlier. Summer is too punctual for an African that one, I thought. Finally, my Friday began.

***

Is she always going to beat me? Just when I thought I was on time, perhaps to settle in nicely before she came through and pick a rather private table that does not attract a lot of attention, there she was, already settled and in her own world. Did she get here thirty minutes before me? This girl is smart.

I took easy steps as I carefully approached the splendour that sat before me. Her beautiful, well-manicured hands rested gracefully on the table; between them rested a box of foreign-looking chocolates. Her head rested peacefully on the back of her chair; was she sitting on her waist? I wondered. On a normal day, that would look like an uncomfortable position, but she looked so peaceful, so free. The fire of passion burned me as I let my eyes indulge in her beauty. But what did I do? I kept asking myself. Linda, the waitress, passed by and gave me that Linda-wink and a friendly smile. I smiled back, and returned my focus to this beautiful being in front of me. I made up my mind right there and then that today I had to do the right thing. I paid attention to her face and realised she had travelled to a place close to heaven if she was not there already. Could it be the chocolate in front of her that had transported her? Summer loved her chocolate too much, and she had great taste too. I could not help myself, but I found my face drawn closer to hers and I kissed her lightly on the forehead. It felt like heaven.

The scent this woman was wearing was so evocative! She slowly opened her eyes and smiled at me. You could see joy run like a river on her face. I am getting lucky, I thought; I must do the right thing today.

"Meditating?" I asked her.

She closed her eyes again and for a moment went back to the place she has been before I made my presence known to her. I wished somebody could confirm for me that she was not human, but an angel. She opened her eyes again, sat up straight and looked at me with hypnotizing eyes.

"Bloody chocolate making love to me," she said.

I didn't mean to laugh at that. I knew she had a sense of humour, but I immediately felt embarrassed and reached for her hand in apology. I must do the right thing today, I thought.

It happened every time we held hands, the connection, the warmth. I felt free, I felt complete. She smiled at me and my shoulders felt light. Then she announced she would visit the bathroom. She had to take her shots, it was 15:30 she reminded me. Once again, the same phrase rang in my mind - I must do the right thing today.

She returned after about five minutes. She looked more determined, more beautiful too. She sat there on her chair like a queen would sit in front of class A commoners. Oh! I love this woman, I thought. She gave me a stern look that had my every fibre bow down to her. I must do the right thing today, I kept telling myself. She stood up, gracefully so, and cleared her throat.

"Let me call you when I get home," she said, when all my attention was captivated, and immediately departed.

That left me numb, disarmed, paralysed; a merciless blow to my face. Was she okay? Did I do something wrong? I tried speaking, but my vocabulary was blank, no words came out of my mouth. I watched her walk away and wished I could stop her, just to make sure she was okay. I tried getting up from my chair but I couldn't, I could not feel my waist or my legs. Tears running down my face as she disappeared from my sight and I could not do anything about it.

What the hell did I do? Too late for the right thing.

A Letter from a Suicide Victim

Ntimana Konyana-Semokonyane

Each and every plan of action has surely had a starting and finishing line. Life is a starting point of the very same journey we are all being entertained in, perhaps we may have different opening lines in our lives, but never mind the choruses; they are only a hullabaloo. Serving with no regard to all these forewords, I conclude with my very own selfishness that we are members of the same force, no matter what.

Hours of my life and my energy I spare, to unfold what is conceived in my life after social-intercourse. It came as a lullaby at first and I couldn't predict what was camouflaged within. As a child, I had always thought so much of the elderly, truly they are smart if only they understand, and not undermine, their capabilities. Living up to being who you really are and exploiting negative minds is actually what I call SMART and what should become of them.

Indifferences rather bittersweet, all the pity you could afford has frankly closed my self survey. A seed of self-pity has been planted in my heart and has germinated into a great harvest. Out of the pity the world grants me there is a huge embargo on existence. I can only sing a bittersweet emotional tune.

I am looking back at the long seconds I have walked with you to come here today. I am extremely sorry to be forced to ask the kind of questions kicking in my mind. It may take 24 hours, but it's a pity I can't wait to get responses. It is about life lived in desire of those who had a choice over my head and heart, yet they are only God's bits of wood like my self.

I am standing in wonderland; am I a mistake or are you a mistake? I don't feel like imagining an answer just in case it only booms in my head. A number of misfortunes have encompassed me up to my last day. Numerous lethal pains I have encountered in tribute to operating what I thought needed amendment. Unfortunate circumstances have made a great indifference dwell in my sanctuary and flash through to the world outside me. My deep sighs add a chill of melancholy and my thoughts are more fierce than mysteries of pain.

Now, I'm on an island of denial and brutality with a quick plan of action. Not so sure whether to show love with respect to your reputation and thoughts. I'm almost totally convinced to put my trust in a passerby who pretends to make my life a priority. I don't deny the fact that you outdid yourself, but another scar on me would be unbearable. You appealed to a sixth sense in me.

As for the end, I don't know when it is to flash. I only wish that I could be done with the miseries and worries pounding my mind. I wish for these semi-filled memories to were occupied with sweet dreams and expectations. May many shiny days glister upon my grave so that my tombstone gives light to those who will still remember my life in celebration. I wish you could accompany me to the end of my breath. Unfortunately you can only stand by my coffin with indecency and cry your victory as though crying my memories.

I don't want to live in your accusation or die a death in your judgment of me. Rather, I want to free your thoughts and help you out of a great evil temptation of reconciliation. Yes, the trash must be thrown away no matter how valuable. Used goods that can't be recycled shouldn't be left around, lest the usable get thrown away in their name. What was I? For unlike energy I am not restorable and not eternal. This is but a resolution to the obstacles so mutual and obvious.

Good things are done for good people by good people. Pity, when wolves in sheep coats beat the good people under the pretence of righteousness. May my hearty apologies get to you and touch your sincerity, allowing you to forgive me from the bottom of your heart. I must have been a great temptation to have prompted your cruelty and heartlessness. I was an evil angel that brought out the animal so wild in you.

That is why with my undying spirit of fighting for fairness and justice I say this prayer for you now and forever more in the depth of my grave and in the mist of creatures of the soil that make a good feast over my voluptuousness.

"Forgive us oh Lord, for we enacted our lustful desires in trespassing against you. Forget the scent of lies and empty promises that only satisfy us and which smell so naturally on us. It is in our ignorance that we tempt our brothers and sisters, that we submit to their heartburns and tears for our victory. You created us so pure but we have surrendered your masterpiece to the evil one. Give us hearts so strong, so that lust and satisfaction don't tempt our will. Put us in the mist of temptations with much armory and make us strong enough to stand firm to accusations untrue!"

And now for those who stay behind, missing my existence, thirsty for my life and success. Will you keep on praying for my redemption from paradise? Your prayers will see me through, though your expectations for my life remain undone. Do not blame him for my death, for my attitude and haste caused the end of my fate. My destiny remains uncovered. I'm so heavy I couldn't win a race against time. Good people just as bad ones are born and ultimately die.

This is where my smiles come to lapse, my dreams are shuttered and expectations stillborn, but at least my pains will heal and I shall never be a victim of any beast's cruel intentions again. Pity I shall not be able to fill the last letters, but all everyone knows is that it is S_ _ _. Sweet or sour? We can not be sure.

Mohla Lineo a Shobelang

Amelia M.

Lineo le Puseletso ba ne ba theohela ka Lekahlong la Kuebunyane moo ba neng ba tsoa isetsa Malome Molefi liperekisi. Ba ne ba tšekalla ba leba motseng oa Kuebung. Ke teng moo ba khahlaneng le Tšupa a ena le metsoalle ea hae Leutsoa le Lebohang. Hobane Lineo le Puseletso ba ne ba tsebana le bahlankana bao, etsoe ba ne ba lula motseng oa Kuebung Ha-Janefeke 'moho, ha baa ka ba ba natsa ha ba ba bona ba atamela ba lebane le bona. Ba mpile ba ba lumelisa ba re: "lumela abuti Tšupa le lona likhaitseli." Boraro boo ke ha bo itsoella pele joalokaha eka ha baa utloa letho.

Lineo le Puseletso ba ile ba makatsoa haholo ke taba eo, empa he ha baa ka ba e touta. Eitse ka mor'a nakoana ba se ba fetane le bashemane bao, keha ba utloa liqi tsa batho ba mathang eka hona le seo ba se balehang li tla li ba labile. Ha ba hetla ho bona na ke'ng e hlahileng ba tsebe ho baleha le bona, keha ba hokomela hore ke Tšupa le metsoalle ea hae, le hore ba ne ba se ba eketsehile ka palo. Hosena ea itseng letho ho e mong, Lineo le Puseletso ba hlanola litlhabela ba khikhithela.

E se neng Tšupa a be a se a qhaulitse Lineo ka letsoho. Puseletso eena a tšaroa ke Rabele, motsoalle oa abuti oa bona ea moholo. Banana bobeli ba lekile ho itharasolla ba ntse ba re "'na ntlohelle". Tšupa le Rabele bona ba re: "ha re ee uena! Ebile ua ntšokolisa ua baleha ha ke tla ho uena?" Ka mantsoe a ntseng a khaoha ke liboko, Puseletso le Lineo ba re: "helang 'na ha ke batle ho tsamaea le uena!" Puo tseo li tsoetse pele joalo bahlankana bao ba babeli ba ntse ba hulanya banana bao joaloka mekotla ea litapole. Har'a tsela keha Rabele a fela pelo eaba oa ema o sheba Puseletso ka mahlong a re ho eena:

"tlohella ho ntšokolisa uena! Ebile kea u tlohella joale, hare ee u itsamaise!" Ha a cho joalo keha a se a kokositse molamu a korotse Puseletso tlhafung ha a ne a ka hana. Rabele: "Heela, hoja ua tsamaea ua tlohella ho ntšenyetsa nako!" Eitse Puseletso a sa ntse a inahana hore na a balehe Rabele a mo tlohetse jooalo, keha mohlankana eo a mo samola 'momo ka lebetlela.

Puseletso a putlama fatše ke bohloko a ba a hoelehetsa a ntša seboko. Ka mor'a moo, letsoalo la ho samoloa hape le ile la mo susumelletsa hore a iqeke a itsamaise joalokaha a ne a laetsoe. Tšupa eena o ne a phathahane ka Lineo a ntse a pheta feela a re: "Heela, ha re tsamaee hle e ntse e ba bosiu!". O ile a hulanya Lineo joalo a sa nke khefu hofihlela a kene ha'bo. Ka mor'a nako e se kae Puseletso le eena o ile a fihla habo mokoeteli oa hae, Rabele. Batho ba motse bona eaba ba iphapantse ha ba ntse ba utloa liboko tsa baroetsana bao seterateng. Ketso ea mofuta ono e ne e se ntho e ncha ho bona. 'M'e oa Rabele le 'Matšupa le bona ba ne ba kene manyalong ka mokhoa o tšoanang, 'me ha baa ka ba Makala ha Rabele le Tšupa ba kena ba hulanya banana bao. Ho fihleng hoa bona, Rabele le Tšupa ba ile ba amoheloa ka mofuthu ke bo 'ma bona. Hanghang keha bo 'M'e matsale bao ba simolla ho lokisetsa lingoetsi tsa bona tse ncha.

Hae ha'bo banana teng ntat'a bona Lefetlama o ne a ntse a ba letile. Ke ho tšoenyeha, keha a ema ka maoto a ea ho metsoalle ea barali bao ba hae na ba ne ba tseba moo ba ileng. E mong oa banana bao a buileng le bona keha a mo tlalehela hore o utloile hothoe Lineo u shobelisitsoe ke Tšupa.

Lefetlama ke ha a tlala-tlala jarete ke bohale. Molekane oa hae 'Matšepo o mo fumane a ntse a jabajaba joalo. "Ekaba molato ke'ng ntate ha u halefile hakaale?": 'Matšepo a botsa. Lefetlama ha a araba a re: "Ke bona eka Motlalepula ha a mpone hohang 'Matšepo! Motlalepula ha a mpone 'Matš epo"

Matšepo: "Ekaba o ents'eng Motlalepula joale 'khetlong lee mohatsa'ka?"

Lefetlama: "Motlalepula o nkile Lineo, 'Matšepo!"

Matšepo: "U bolela'ng ha u re Motlalepula o nkile Lineo?"

Lefetlama ka lentsoe le phefa le futhang ka khalefo a re: "Ke re Motlalepula o nkile Lineo! Ha u utloe ka litsebeng? Motlalepula o nkile thepa eaka a sa nkopa, a sa mpatala. Motlalepula o nkutsoelitsi 'Matšepo!"

Ka mor'a ho thola nakoana, 'Matšepo a tsoela pele a re: "E le hore u bolela hore Lineo o shobelisitsoe ntate?".

Lefetlama ke ha a mo kharumela a re: "Ke cho joalo, u nts'o sa nkutloe!"

'Matš epo a botsa ka boikokobetso hore na Puseletso eena o kae hobane o ne a tsamaile 'moho le Lineo. Mothating ono Lefetlama o ne a se a kene tseleng a tatile, 'me a hloloa ho ananela potso ea mosali oa hae eo a neng a mo setse morao ka potlako.

Matšepo: "Joale u ea kae ntate re ntse re bua?"

Lefetlema: "Ke ilo lata thepa eaka!". Ho fihleng hoa hae ha Motlalepula ntat'a Tšupa, Lefetlema ke ha a fothola lemati la moo la lesenke a sa kokota, a ba a batla a le roba. Ha a kena ka hare ke ha a thulana le Tšupa a ntse a ja papa ea mabela eaba o mo naumela ka molamu. Rao! Setulong, ke ha Tšupa a qoba ka sefutho. Lefetlama a bua ka khalefo a re: "Moshanyana tooe oa seburabura, tlisa ngoana'ka. U mo isitse kae?".

Pele Tšupa a ka araba, ntata'e Motlalepula le mosali'ae ba be se ba le teng. Motlalepula a re: "Butle Lefetlama, ha ho ke ho etsoe tjena mora monna. Litaba lia buisanoa, li shebisanoe. Theola moea Motlokoa re tsebe ho bua". Eaka a ka be a sa cho joalo, Lefetlema a araba a re: "ha e'ka u ntse u ntella ho ea pele tjee Motlalepula? U nkile thepa eaka re sa rerisana, joale u boetse u eketsa Batlokoa ka 'na!".

Motlalepula: "Thupa ha e shape fatše hle mohaisane, 'M'e ke 'M'ao hle ngoan'eso, ha re lule fatše re buisane."

Lefetlama: "U re 'M'e ke 'm'ao? Ehlile tello ea hau ke e se nang moeli Motlalepula! 'M'e haa tsoala lirathana tse kang uena tjena keo joetse Motlalepula. 'M'ao e keke ea'ba 'm'ak'a le khaale!"

Lefetlama o bobile feela mohlang ho buang mosali'ae 'Matšepo ha a re: butle ntat'a Lineo seke oa re tlontlolla tjena. Hase uena feela ea lahlehetsoeng mona."

Ka morao hore malapa ao a mabeli a rarolle litaba, ba ile ba arohana ka le reng lelapa la Motlalepula le tla itlaleha ha Lefetlama e se neng, 'me tebello e ne e le hore ba tla mo hlatsoa matsoho. Litumellano tseno li ile tsa khotsofatsa Lefetlama leha e ne e se ka botlalo.

Ha ba tloha ha Motlalepula, 'Matšepo le Lefetlama ba ile ba leba ha bo Rabele ho fapana le ho ea hae. Ba ne ba utloetse hona ha Motlalepula hore Puseletso o moo. Ntat'a Rabele e ne e se e le mofu empa Rangoana'e o ile a 'muelella. Malapa a ile a fihlella litumellano 'me ba arohana ka khotso.

Ho ile hoa hlaka ka morao hore Lefetlama o ne a halefisitsoe ke hore barali ba hae ha baa kuptjoa ho eena ka sebele, eseng ha kaalo-kaalo hore ba se ba nyetsoe. Mokhoa oa hae e ne e le motho ea sa rateng ho telloa.

Ka mor'a hore Tšupa a lokolleloe mosali oa hae ka molao, ke ha a kena ka tlung a re o il'o ba le eena. Lineo eena hang ha a 'mona o ile a nyekeloa ke pelo, a senyeha maikutlo. Mahlong a Lineo, Tšupa e ne e le mohlankana a bolelele bo sa khahlising, a motšo ba seqo se cheleng, meno a hae a le masehla a botša ho se hlatsuoe, ha nko eona e ne e ka sehloba se opeloang.

Ka lehlohonolo Lineo e ne e le ngoanana ea kelello e chorileng. Hanghang ke ha a loa leqheka eaba o re ho Tšupa: "Butle ho hlobola, ke kopa u mphelehetse ke utloa ke hloka ho ea matlapeng." Tšupa o ile a lumela. Ha ba fihla moo matlapeng, Lineo a kopa ho theohela pejana moo a neng a batla ho itšireletse ka lefikana leo a neng a le bona. Monghali a boetse a lumela.

Bonneteng Tšupa o ne a belaela hore Lineo o batla ho baleha empa o ne a tšepile lintja tsa motse hobane a tseba hore li kholo ebile li bohale. O ne a itšelisa ka hore Lineo a keke a ba le sebete sa ho ropoha feela har'a bosiu bo bokaalo a le mong.

Hang hoba a theohele moo Tšupa a sa 'moneng, ke ha a itahla Lineo a phaphatheha ngoan'e mosehla. O mathile joalo a khetha tsela eo a tsebang hore ho eona a keke a hlahella ho moo Tšupa a neng emeng teng. Ha Lineo a kenelletse motseng hantle o ile a kokota ntlong ea pele eo a khahlaneng le eona. Ha batho ba moo ba bula o ile a kopa thuso, empa moo a reng o ba joetsa 'nete o ile a koeneha. Lineo o ile a hopola hore ba tloha ba mo khutlisitsa morao moo a tsoang teng ba re ke lehlanya la ngoanana le balehang lenyalo. Kahoo, o ile a khetha ho ba joetsa hore o phirimalletsoe 'me o kopa ho felehetsoa hobane o tšaba lintja.

Ha a se a fuoe moshanyana oa lapeng leo hore a mo felehetsa Lineo keha a mo kopa hore ba tsamaee ka tsela e sa feteng pel'a hab'o Tšupa. Ba tsamaile hantle hofihlela ba kena lapeng habo. Kapele-pele keha Lineo a potlakela ho kokota ntlong eo 'M'ae le ntata'e ba robalang ho eona. Hoba a hlolose hore eena haa batle ho nyaloa ke Tšupa, 'm'ae ke ha a itšoara hloohong a tapatapa fatše a re: "Ekaba ngoana eo o nkutloang Molimo oaka ha a tlo ntlotlolla ha kale? Lineo! Lineo! ua hlanya Lineo? U re ha u batle ho nyaloa? Jonna ke tsoetse sehole oe!"

Lefetlama le eena li kena: "Batšoeneng ba ntsoetseng, ekaba ke hlaheloa keng! Lineo e le hore ha u le tje u balehile lenyalong?"

Ka mantsoe ao le a mang a latetseng, batsoali ba Lineo ba ile ba mo akhella matsoho eaba ba qetella ka hore moshanyana eo a neng a mo felehelitse a mo khutlisetsa hab'o Tšupa. Ba chulo joale ba bile ba koala lemati. Lineo o ile a sareloa haholo empa a se lahle tšepo. O ile a kopa eena moshanyane eo a neng a ntse a tsamaea le eena hore a mo ise ha maloma'e Molefi moo a neng a etetse teng motšeare. Ka Lehlohonolo moshanyana eo o ile a mo ananela eaba ba leba motseng oa Kuebenyane. Ha ba fihla teng, Lineo o ile a buleloa ke eena maloma'e ka sebele. Ha Molefi a bona Lineo a seka meokho, o ile a ameha haholo le eena eaba o re ho eena: "thola nkhono, s'ka lla, U bolokehile mona".

Ka mor'a ho se lumellane ka maikutlo le batsoali ba hae, Lineo o ile a qetella a se a lula ha maloma'e Molefi hofihlela a qetile lithuto. O ile a pasa Form E ka sehlopha sa pele ebile e le moithuti oa pele oa ho pasa hantle hakaalo sekolong sa hae. O ile a tsoela pele a ithuta molao sekolong se seholo sa sechaba moo le teng a ileng a pasa ka linaleli. Ha a qeta moo, Lineo o ile a tsoela pele ka lithuto tsa hae Kapa naheng ea Aforeka Boroa, moo kajeno a sebetsang e le leqoetha.

Puseletso eena hoba a kene lenyalong, o ile a khaohana le lithuto. Batsoali ba bona ba se ba fetotse mecha joale hobane Lineo o atlehile. Ba ithorisa ka eena ebile ha ba qete ho bua ka eena. Leha ho le joalo, Lineo o se a sa etela hae hangata haesale maloma'e Molefi a hlokahala. O mo hopola ka mehla hobane hoja maloma'e a s'a lumela ho bokhoni ba hae a ba a mo fa monyetla, Lineo a ka be a se moo a leng teng kajeno.

The North Beckons

Wolf

It's good to be home. No it's great to be home, like Andy Dufresne from Shawshank Redemption spreading his arms in the rain after he makes his escape – like a man freed from prison and headed for paradise. He also had to have the faecal matter washed off so I guess there's that too. Anyways that's not the point. My Andy Dufresne moment comes when I hear everyone around me speak in my beautiful mother tongue; the melodic Sesotho. Even the occasional exhortation for me to get out of the way by passersby, *"Tlohella ho peralla ka tseleng, re soaele re tatile. Koloi lia re siea!"* will not sway me. I'm home. Everywhere inside this landlocked mountain kingdom is home.

Downtown Maseru this afternoon is as buzzing as can be. Bustling with activity at every turn and delivering my senses to a rebirth. I can taste the specks of the August dust on my lips, Bhudaza's *BoMapefane* is playing in my ears as I make my way to the taxi rank, the saxophone serenading every scene my eyes breathe in. How fitting? I am after all on my way to Leribe district, Lisemeng. The oldest part of the biggest town in the north – Hlotse which is also Bhudaza's hometown. This a town I've carried with me everywhere I went, this is why I root for the Starks on Game of Thrones and my spirit animal is a wolf. While my north's mascot is a buffalo and when Linare football club plays, I've opted for the Wolf alter ego because unlike buffaloes, wolves can thrive in cold solitude and this is a state I've mostly found myself in for the past 6 years. Our Leribe slogan – *Ke tla leka joalo ka nare* which translates to *I'll try like a buffalo* has been my life motto; resilience. I've carried it with me like a Zulu warrior does his spear. Resilience and the fear of losing hope have been my driving force for years. But now

I'm in the capital, Maseru –it's a perfect prelude to my prodigal return.

On my way from the border I saw places that were pregnant with memories of a ripe and naïve adolescence – LNDC complex was where I had my first date with a girl who, funny enough, delivered my first heartbreak. The Standard Bank - Tower Branch further up Kingsway road on the right is where my childhood best friend's father worked or maybe still works. We used to crush about four *Hall's* menthols each to mask the Courtleigh cigarette scent before we met him, whenever I'd come to Maseru. It was only now that I realised how much of me was in this city, something I had never cared to look into. Queen Elizabeth II hospital rests on the right before we turn left, I had my first HIV/AIDS test in 2009 – I was still a virgin so the whole process was uneventful, wish I could say the same right now.

I'm taking all these sights in while lodged between two middle-aged women in the backseat of a *4+1* taxi. One of them was furiously indulging in a fried russian whose scent filled the beaten up Corolla, the very serpent in my Eden – I did not miss this scent. I get off at Sefika complex and walk all the way to Pitso ground to board the Quantum to Maputsoe. I finally get to see Sefika High School, from where one of my best friends and brother got his *Top Ten*-laced grade 12 COSC certificate. Famo music plays from the various hawker stalls and supermarket *stoeps* all the way to the taxi rank. This of course could be heard in between Bhudaza. The bag that has been heavy on my back all the way across South Africa is weightless in the presence of my people. Every single one of them walking past me bears the very blood that flows through me. Back in Ankara, where I now reside, me and my friends used to tell kids from other countries that being from a Kingdom, our blood was relatively royal and that they should afford us some respect. This memory crosses my mind and leaves behind a nostalgic smirk on my fiercely dark face.

I pay 20 Rands more for the Quantum ride than the last time I was home. *Mohlomong ke lekhetho,* seeing how long it's been since I was home, but no, I've had both the Kingdom and Leribe in me since the day I left. I brush the price increase-infused guilt off as I squeeze through to my seat. I claim the seat before the back row, for a guy who weighs 60kg, this is not bad – to be seated on what's know as the *toilet.* This brings back memories, high school memories, of all those trips we took to debate tournaments. I went to a predominantly middle class high school, at least by Lesotho's standards. Inside the Quantum is a myriad of classes and yet we're all connected by the same ethnicity. Ethnicity and race are words I'd learned once I had left the womb of Africa – I'd always thought we were all, to an extent, one, but your world taught me even people fall into different classes. This has been a bittersweet lesson, but aren't all real life lessons?

In the Quantum, it is a further breath of fresh air hearing my mother tongue spoken from seat to seat, by those occasionally taking phonecalls and from the Pioneer speakers from whence a Moafrika FM radio presenter reads the 1 pm news. Something weird happens after the news is read, something called *Pitsa Ea Litutla* is advertised and this sparks a conversation amongst the passengers; some doubt its authenticity and a man all the way from the front seat says he would not advise anyone to trust the radio station owner Professor Sebonomoea. It's hard to listen to what he's saying because he takes intermitent sips of Bibo as he speaks. I didn't even think they still sold those and why did anyone act like Sebonomoea was a name you hear every day? I think it roughly translates to 'a fart' or maybe they did hear it every day. I immediately zone out of this conversation when my eyes fall on the outline of the still snow-capped Maluti range on the left of the Main North 1. A symbolic sight, as if to welcome back the prodigal son, we had just crossed the Phuthiatsana River and are officially in the north, Leribe.

Now that I'm breathing all this in after being away from home, in Ankara for five years on an scholarship, it's insanely infuriating thinking of how Western media portrays us. It is nothing less than "Africa – One Country." I spend most of my time in Ankara explaining to non-believing strangers how their country was not the first place I encountered clothing, lions do not roam willy nilly in Lesotho and that there is peace in my country. How could a country this multifaceted in its beauty be drowned in one vile, stereotype shamelessly devoid of any truth? In 45 minutes, I have already experienced incredible sensations no other country in the world, the whole of Africa included, can ever give you. Leribe my first love, I missed you anyway.

Summer in the South

K. Phenduka

The football field still retains its size, a little green on the one end and dusty ground on the other. Together with the fields surrounding it they had seen a match now and then, eavesdropped on the young lovers in their night strolls as they promised each other things out of their reach and at times it had been a host to the local gatherings called on by both the chief and those of the demagogic politicians who forever promised the villagers a tarred road from the border post to the main road.

The now deserted village had at one point many a people; a chief in whom the villagers had unshakeable confidence, footless young ones chasing each other up and down the rocky village passages, a village tap which on approach of dusk entertained those in their teens years as boys made attempts at winning the hearts of the firm breasted girls washing moroho, by either carrying many water buckets or reciting heartfelt praises to their desired lovers. The fields, now naked and dry, were arable, thus a source of good food for the village. It was peaceful and welcoming, all seemed to be going well for everyone. All these were now tales recited by the few who remained, at night to the little ones. Urbanization had invaded the village, taking with it the villagers as spoils. Some had permanently moved whilst others still visited during the year and December holidays. Summer holidays in December now bring back many memories and the village vibe, the football field, the village tap, the local tavern and some houses for a few weeks regain their triumph.

In the mountainous country of Lesotho, on the southern side, in the district of Quthing, is where this awe-inspiring village is found. Situated near the border between Lesotho and South Africa it is engulfed by the waters of the mighty Senqu River and the enigmatic Tele River, with only a graveled road deviating from the main road zigzagging to the border post like a python. This village is the birthplace of both Mncedisi's mother and grandfather and like them he had partly grown up in it. Summertime by the rock where initiated men would sit, playing Morabaraba as their mouths turned chimneys puffed on either BB or Boxer, tobacco that is still typical here, he sits with his brothers and they reminisce about their years growing up, laugh at their foolish deeds and victories. The village has now changed, thus they no longer have as many friends as they had back then, separated by walks of life and aspirations. Despite this it is still pleasing that they gather here at this time of the year.

At night in the lounge they assemble, Tatu mkhulu Velaphi sipping on his class of whisky, the expression on his face declaring his satisfaction. His children and grandchildren all vanish the whole year, and customarily around this time his two houses forget tranquility and silence and get filled with his offspring and rowdy grandchildren. On their first night at home their conversation with the old man mostly pertains to what has happened in their long absence around the village, the herding of the sheep and goats, their progeny, the field produce and plans for the coming year. The old man rarely inquires about their lives in the different cities from which they all earn a living. The kitchen exhales mouth-watering aromas as the women prepare supper; for Mncedisi it feels good to be home.

In the early morning hours the village cocks crow consecutively like an organized parade. The sun is not yet up but darkness has disappeared. Mncedisi walks to the kraal and inspects the sheep whilst attending to nature's call, feeling so wonderfully positive. The sheep wait in enthusiasm for the shepherd and his appearance shutters their keen anticipation, for they know their leader. The chief's sheriff stands by the hill and delivers announcements from the chief and the sun emerges from the mountain giving light and life to the village. Unlike in winter, only a few bask in the sun, since it is already warm and on its summer appearance is too hot. The village women are about to finish sweeping in their yards and those already done fill the fresh morning breeze with smoke as they prepare meals for shepherds and their households.

Mncedisi's whole family is up. Everybody is allocated a task and at approximately 10:00 am Aba Kwa Nxumalo gather in the kitchen for breakfast. The day passes and the time most awaited by those in their twenties arrives. After supper, Mncedisi, along with Mzoxolo and Sipho, his elder brothers, sneak out of their dark bedroom and go to the local bar for a few cold ones. Inside, Famo music plays at a low volume thus allowing the customers to indulge in conversations. A man neatly dressed dances on the open floor alone and ladies ululate as he moves his shoulders back and forth in rhythm with the song.

They settle in one of the groups and here a proposition is put forth, young men in their early twenties stone it with harsh rebuttals, some logical and some in all material aspects fallacious. It had by now become a ritual to discuss issues amongst themselves, some were of paramount significance whilst others were trivial, still, no matter how sensitive, realistic or controversial, the issue of the hour would enjoy a suitable analysis.

At times the arguing becomes ad-hominem, but this does not thwart the boys. Their topics, always intriguing in nature, enjoy an array of listeners along. Funny how they still maintain their friendships, yet they have a number of differences and diverse approaches to living. Do they share a common goal, vision, aspiration? Or are they just chatty quarrelers? This has never been divulged nor can be inferred.

From their debates, they have come to learn and appreciate that in their dealings with human beings it should constantly be borne in mind that human beings are not creatures of logic, but are bred creatures of emotions, an aspect which many have grown oblivious of. The cold and refreshing drinks keep coming, the boys sit and the debate keeps intensifying.

More men and women join in on the dance floor and attempts are made to emulate the neatly dressed man who was still dancing. The dancing halts their debate as some of the boys in their circle join in on the dancing too and as a result a request for increased volume is made. At this time of the year one would say the villagers, especially the youths, have inscripted in their hearts the words unearthed amongst the remains of the once flourishing Roman colony Timgad which proclaim, "hunting, bathing, playing and laughing" to be living, an assertion which many may dare to challenge. Revelry, good food, and laughing are daily to them.

A Famo love song begins and those on stage grab their mates. Surprisingly, amongst the couples on the dance floor, is one detested by many elders in the village. It is Lipuo a wealthy woman in her early thirties and Mokopu a lad in his twenties. Of their newfound relationship, Mncedisi has in the last few hours learnt that it has been a spark of many hullabaloos in the village. Some alleging she is exploiting her young lover with her riches whilst some assume she has visited the local witch doctor and requested a remedy commonly known as *sheba nna feela* (fix your gaze at me alone), to use on this young man. In here at night unlike in daylight they openly display their affection for each other and they dance together whilst Mokopu sings to her parts of the song. Mncedisi intently looks at them and they unexpectedly trigger memories of Disraeli, one of the great state men and earl of England and Marry Anne a wealthy woman, who like these two were in a relationship similar in nature. Mncedisi recalls how historians and novels proclaim Marry Anne to have lived for her young lover alone and he comes to conclude that maybe like Marry Anne, Lipuo knows the art of handling men.

A hand firmly grasps his shoulder; promptly his archaic thoughts disappear as he turns around to find Nomthandazo warmly smiling at him. All of a sudden his mouth gets dry, his heart starts palpitating and words vanish into thin air. She had only said she is arriving today; he did not anticipate that she would pursue to see him on the very day of her arrival. Locked in a gaze, he wishes to tell her of the thoughts that torture his relentless mind. They hug and catch the attention of the crowd. As an endeavor to avoid further stares he takes her hand and they march outside. The warm summer breeze welcomes them outside and the moon is mesmerized by the sudden appearance of these two lovebirds.

They walk past the old store, which was at once the hub of trade to all the surrounding villages, from Sixondo to Seaka. Many would come here for their household's necessities. They walk through the football pitch, strolling to her grandfather's hut, where he bids her farewell the way lovers do, and then he depart for the bar.

Back at the bar, police officers have raided the area, vehemently ordering people to go home. In the mist of the complaining mob, Mncedisi spots his brothers who were also on the lookout for him. They laugh at his glowing look and walk home whilst mocking him. Once in his old squeaky bed, Mncedisi gets lost in thoughts of his dear Nomthandazo.

It is not peculiar in the village to find old men in their homes settled under a tree's shade engaging in a soliloquy whilst puffing on a Boxer filled pipe. Some famo singers have come to make songs of this odd behavior, asserting that as the old man sits there, his pipe oozing infinitely, he is meditating and scrutinizing lofty issues. The older women, in contrast to their devotees, usually indulge in long conversations about incidents in their community and the neighboring ones. Summertime makes this privilege easier as they are cut from their chores by either their daughters or grandchildren, and they therefore get to mingle and talk more. Unlike the rest of the year where they only get to chat while collecting wood, now they get to make homely visits and gossip thoroughly as they enjoy coffee or a cold drink and at times they send kids on an errands to get a few quarts for them at the local bar.

A few households are still blessed with some cattle, sheep, goats and donkeys. At his house Mr. Velaphi has since his retirement from the Gold Fields mines in South Africa, managed to get a few goats for his kraal which he claims was once filled with many a cows. Mncedisi has generally never been very fond of livestock, and the old man still shouts at him for his infatuation with books. After all, a man's beauty as the old believe, is his ability to possess a vast herd of livestock. Mr. Velaphi still holds a firm belief in the principles instilled in him in his growth and he has exhausted his efforts to inculcate them in all of his children and grandchildren. However, his efforts have unfortunately yielded poorly since his house is filled with bookworms.

Nevertheless, Mr. Velaphi still vehemently emphasizes that it is constructive for the boys to drive the goats to the open grazing areas for summer. Mncedisi and his brothers, along with other boys from the village, take their herds out all night and bring them back in the morning hours after sunrise. They prepare for this in various ways and each year they view the summer sunrise from the mountaintop as the animals graze. The experience is finalized by a walk back to their differing homes, a moment which has come to be Mncedisi's most preferred. Each year on this walk, clouded by silence, he reflects on his achievements that year and makes his resolutions for the future.

'Mamotimpana

Selloane Tseka

'Mamotimpana was the type of a friend whom no parent wished their child to be associated with. Whether my own family really saw what she was like or chose to ignore her is a total mystery to me. I never got around to finding out how she got the name, but I know it had a lot to do with her looks. She was very tall for her age; her skin was so dark it shone. Her muscular physique, which resembled that of a racehorse, made her a magnet for a lot of names like 'axe head,' 'giraffe,' and 'black panther,' which were whispered in secret. No one in their right mind wanted to be involved in a fight with her; she fought like an angry gorilla. Everyone, especially boys whose egos would hurt more than bruises, gave her a wide berth.

One fine day a short skinny boy whom everyone called 'City' made the mistake of calling her 'Black Goliath.' I don't know if he was trying to test the waters to see what would happen or he was just plain stupid. We were all having lunch in the school hall when the words were spoken. As everyone turned their eyes towards 'Mamotimpana, I dug into my soup not daring to look at her face. When I finally did, she was completely calm and expressionless. This surprised me a great deal, especially when the boy started laughing loudly with two of his friends and patting each other on the back. Still, 'Mamotimpana remained calm and ate her soup. This both surprised and worried me; it was totally unlike her to leave such a crime unpunished.

Days, and then weeks passed with the incident forgotten until one Monday during break. Near the boys toilets a crowd was gathering and a boy was screaming. Rushing to see what was happening, I found 'Mamotimpana with her hand between City's legs, squeezing. City, who was rather light-skinned was slowly turning purple. Everyone was giggling; not even lifting a finger to help. "Who is Black Goliath *uena*? I will pull out this small thing and send it to the holy land," 'Mamotimpana was saying as she slowly twisted her hand. City started to neigh like a stallion back in the village with his eyes bulging out of his small head. His nightmare ended with the bell announcing the end of break. From that day onwards, City walked with downcast eyes and was not his usual talkative self.

'Mamotimpana's ridiculous and daring self made me nervous all the time, and for some reason I was always around when she exercised her creativity. She and her aunt did not get along at all. One afternoon I visited 'Mamotimpana's home and I found her stirring something vigorously in a pot on an open fire, beads of sweat forming on her forehead from the exertion and the heat. Curious, I asked what was in the pot and she answered, "Some meat for that hag. I have to cook hers aside as she doesn't take any salt with her food." I commented that it must taste awful. She took a piece of meat from the pot, blew it to cool it off and threw it in her mouth, chewed and spat it back out shaking her head. "It tastes like a dog's butt; I don't know how anyone can live off something like this." Then she continued stirring. I looked around nervously, afraid that someone might have seen her spit the meat. Seeing my discomfort, she spooned some up and started yelling, "*Mosakaso! Mosakaso!*" Mosakaso was a neighbor's dog with black matted fur so scrawny he looked like he was walking sideways. On this occasion, he emerged, wagging his thin tail. I could only gape in horror as he was given the meat and left to lick the spoon clean! Then the spoon went back into the pot to resume its duty. Yes, that was my friend, always scaring me to death with her appalling and disgraceful tactics.

In those days, water was not as accessible as it is today. The village

187

had one rusty water pump that you had to work on for at least an hour before any water came out. Sometimes as if to spite us, it would break down. Our only source of water was a spring which was in the next village. Getting water from there was not an easy task, especially when the occupants rose at the crack of dawn to collect the clean water, leaving us murky dregs which were so hard to reach that one had to kneel and bend in a v-like shape until their butt was pointing to the sky.

One a woman from our village made the mistake of leaving her clean water unattended in a drum before 'Mamotimpana and I came to do laundry. At first, we decided that the murky water from the spring will have to do, but after going on our knees several times and emerging with bucketfuls of water that seemed to get only dirtier, 'Mamotimpana had had enough! She went to the drum of clear water and scooped a bucketful, and then another until the drum was only a quarter full. She then skipped about doing laundry with clean water. I, on the other hand, was so scared I kept glancing around for the drum's owner to appear at any time. When a stout woman finally appeared with a basket of dirty laundry balanced on her head, I was praying silently to the holy mother that she was not the owner of the water. My heart jumped into my throat as she went straight to the drum! I whispered, "She's here." 'Mamotimpana didn't even look in the woman's direction and kept on washing.

Because I could not relax, I kept glancing at the woman from the corner of my eye. First, she looked in the drum, frowned, looked around a bit more, and then gave us a look so cold it could have frozen hell to its core. "What is she looking at? We didn't take her water *rona*!" 'Mamotimpana mumbled as I swallowed what felt like a dry brick and tried to avert my eyes from the woman. Moments later I was startled by the sound of splashing water; the woman was roughly swooshing water from the well with her bucket and throwing it in her drum, all the time giving us a judgmental look. When she was finally done, she stripped down to her nightdress, which had the look of worn out curtains, then started stomping on her laundry to wash it. Seeing this, I pursed my lips to stop the laughter, which was threatening to come out of my ears. 'Mamotimpana however, did not try so hard. She threw her head back and laughed so hard her shoulders were shaking. Then, as if talking to me, she said, "My friend, are you sure you sleep in those rags? *Ache*! Your panties are so old, I am sure you are afraid to put them out on the line with your other clothes." With that, she clapped her hands. By then, I couldn't help myself, and the laughter which had been welling up and choking me, came out in torrents. As I started cackling away like a crazy hyena, the woman kept on doing her laundry as if she didn't even hear us.

Unfortunately, not all of 'Mamotimpana's victims were as aloof as that woman. One very hot afternoon we were seated outside her house under the shade of a tree when four grotesque-looking boys our age happened to pass by. One was wearing shorts that had two oval shaped holes at the back, revealing his chalky buttocks, which looked like they had not had a smear of Vaseline in over a decade. This time, 'Mamotimpana caught me unaware as she yelled, "Some people's buttocks! It is like they use them to wipe the floor! The funny thing is that they are not even nice enough to greet us, yet they look like baboons from the back." This, she said loudly enough for them to hear. The boys wasted no time as they immediately turned around. Seeing this, 'Mamotimpana ran inside her house and I heard a loud click as she locked the door. Having nowhere to run, I decided to remain where I was and keep my cool, though my heart was banging so loudly I was scared it would explode. I was prayed fervidly that the boys would lose their nerve and go away, but I gave up as they came in through the gate.

They were even more frightful looking up close. Their dark faces, which were contorted in anger, reminded me of creatures of the night. "Where did your friend go?" asked the one with torchlights on his butt. I tried to answer, but fear had my throat clenched tight so I simply looked around and shrugged instead. "What were you saying about us?" Asked the tallest boy, who was wearing a coat so crumbled it looked like a cow had chewed on it and spat it out. I started squirming like a trapped mouse and swallowed hard, as my eyes searched for a way to escape. "Hello, how can we help you gentlemen?" said a familiar voice as 'Mamotimpana's aunt appeared from the back of the house. "We were just asking for directions and we found help, thank you," answered the tallest boy baring his big yellow teeth. With that, he gave me a "this is not over" look and they all left. Later, 'Mamotimpana appeared laughing her cheeks off once again.

'Mamotimpana and I had plenty of adventures growing up, and because she did not get along with anyone else, I ended up being her only friend. I believed that the tribulations of life would see her change and become a completely different person, but I realized some things never change when years later, I showed her my boyfriend's picture and she said, "*Mannyeo* why does he look like he fell off a horse? I have never seen such an ugly person in my life!"

Triumphant Battles

Mojabeng Moholi

Summer rains have always been my weakness, the smell of fresh soil as the sky waters hit the earth. The kind of ambrosia that can get one going for days. There is only one thing that ever got me crazy to the core when it rained. Our family had to shift all the furniture in the house the put buckets on the empty side. My twin sister and I would then play our little indoor "mankokosane" up until we drained all our energy to sleep. One thing about growing up with nothing is that you learn to appreciate everything, even the smallest sunsets, especially when you have another half to get up to no good with.

Lindiwe was my identical twin. We grew up in the beautiful valleys of Ha Matela, Morija. The best part about growing up was when we would climb up the hills and watch our brother and father heard the chief village cows. On the hill we would pick up some traditional moroho, so that our mother would have something to cook. Sometimes our brother Mpho would climb with us and hunt wild rabbits. We would keep the wild rabbits for Sunday when mother was off from work. This was because she would make a really delicious stew that would last for a couple of days.

According to my family's tradition, my sister and I had to be separated. This was after we both fell from a tree at the same time while picking berries. We had wanted to pick berries for mother to make a delicious jam so that we would not be stuck with horrible plain bread and fouro juice. Scientifically, it made sense why the branch broke and fell. The branch was overwhelmed with both our masses therefore, it had to give in. It is a pity the village people were filled with such creepy superstitions. What did we know we were just kids.

The day of the separation arrived. I sat there and watched my best friend being taken away from me. The day was filled with a lot of ceremonies and then when I wasn't watching my sister was taken away by relatives who lived in Maseru. This happened when I was 7 years old. For weeks I couldn't sleep, eat or play. The only thing I did was sit in a corner and cry. I blamed myself for being selfish on the day of the accident. Lindiwe did not even like jam she would say it tasted too sweet. As time passed on I carried this deep immense hatred for myself. As I grew into being a teenager I wanted nothing to do with the village and its horrible superstitions.

The truth is that Morija can not even be considered much of a village as it is one of the main tourist attractions in the country. Yet I was filled with so much hate for the minds of my family. Over the years I saw my sister only on holidays and some weekends. One thing I can tell you and that is that Lindiwe's remorse was far greater than that I had harbored in my heart, it was intense to an extent that a psychologist would say she had depression.

Immediately after high school my sister and I had made a pact to apply for scholarships away from Lesotho. Having made this promise, I made sure to get a top three pass from Morija Girls High school and was accepted into the University of Botswana. It is funny how life sometimes plays out. My sister went to University of Botswana the same year and she was able to get us scholoarship because she had exposure to big things such as internet cafés and extensive NGO offices.

My background served as the basis for the degree I wanted to pursue because I did not want anyone to become a victim of the mitosis my sister and I went through. Therefore, I choose social psychology and genetics as my majors, while my sister choose medicine, and my brother choose animal science and soil engineering.

The first few years in Botswana ware difficult; the heat, people and the language were all like a hard jigsaw puzzle. The main thing that kept us going was the motivational words from our struggling parents and having to understand ourselves, where we came from, and the bright future we both had.

In my fourth year I failed one module so I had to pay the fees on my own. Varsity in a foreign country was not smooth sailing. I tried applying for a job, but I failed so I opted for being a charity case which really hurt my pride. Most days I would go into Lindiwe's room and stay with her which was totally against the rules, but no one could tear us apart..Some nights I would sleep in the hospitals quarters where Lindiwe worked and pretend to be her. My sister and I were still living on the twin edge also known as double identity saga. Yes, I know it was not wise for me to spend all of my allowance and internship money, but no one thinks they are going to fail one module and end up being homeless.

After six months was over I finally got a job as a first year genetics tutor, and as a waitress in a restaurant on weekends. I was always a clumsy scatterbrain, but it's funny how some schedules can allow your brain to get adjusted and become the best person you can. In December, it was finally time to write exams. Lindiwe and I had planned to go gallivanting around the streets of Gaborone after we had completed our exams. Yet, just after writing, I fainted at the door of the exam hall.

Three hours later I woke up in hospital filled with tubes all over my body. "Lindiwe is that you?" I heard as a nurse walked towards me holding a series of tubes and paper. I smiled at her and tried explaining I was not Lindiwe, but Thandiwe. Lindiwe and I had few friends so not many people at the hospital knew she was a twin. The nurse asked a series of questions. I knew I had to come clean about a series of headaches I had been having, but I had to make her vow not to tell my overprotective twin. Later that day the nurse and doctors took me to an MRI and CTI scans. The scan revealed a series of unexpected horrors. The doctor told me I had a brain tumor and that it crossed the blood brain barrier. The news crushed me tremendously. I was not upset that I was in pain, but I thought of my sister and family. I had promised Lindiwe I would be with her forever. Eventually, I was released from the hospital after the doctor and I had scheduled surgery and radiotherapy.

The moment of truth settled upon me. The treatment was horrible. Days of needles and endless scans took a toll on me to the point where I was not able to return home for the holidays. I needed my family to support me, but I had told them lies about why I had not come home. The truth was that I wanted to buy time to become better,,not shower them with bad news of how I had a tumor.

By January my treatment was over and I had made a miraculous recovery. The first week of January I went back home and shattered the vessel news I had been carrying a few weeks prior. A sway of relief passed over me as though a large weight had been lifted from my shoulders and chest. During my visit home however I my nose started bleeding and I began spitting small fragments of tissues in my mouth. Lindiwe was an advanced medical student by then and she knew spitting tissue is never a good indication. So my family rushed me to Scott Hospital in Morija.

Lindiwe used to volunteer at this hospital during the holidays so she knew most of the doctors. Fortunately one of our neighbours Thato was a doctor on call that day and she was a specialist in oncology. Despite the fact that Scott Hospital did not have fancy equipment, Lindiwe and Thato did the best they could until I could be transferred to a better facility where I was completely healed from my cancer.

Writer biographies

'Mantšabeng Lifalakane Tuoane

'Mant'sabeng Lifalakane is currently an Assistant Economic Planner in the Ministry of Gender, Youth, Sports and Recreation. She has got a keen interest in Sesotho and English literature as well as storytelling. She also has very serious interest in the rights of disadvantaged groups. It was in this capacity that she became an executive member of a newly found NGO: Centre for Constitutional Human Rights Watch.

Mrs. Lifalakane is a graduate of the National University of Lesotho where she received a BA in Economics and a minor in Statistics. Her specific areas include strategic planning, physical and financial reporting, budgeting, evaluating and monitoring projects. After graduation, Mrs Lifalakane became an active youth leader in the Lesotho Girl Guides Association (LGGA) where she volunteered to teach Life Skills and HIV/AIDS education around High Schools in Berea in a project that was funded by UNICEF; after which, she worked as a Mathematics teacher in Koeneng High School where she also became a coordinator of the school's cultural group.

'Masello Constancia Sello

'Masello was born in the district of Thaba-Tseka but bred in the capital of Maseru. She started her journey of education in 2001 at Seboka Primary School and furthered her education at Mabathoana High School in 2008. She is currently doing her Diploma in Business Management at Lerotholi Polytechnic (Fokothi) and is in her second year. She is a second born and she is currently raised by her single mother after losing her father in 2011.

Masello, a bit of an introvert, enjoys reading at leisure time. She believes books are her solace in life when she is at her lowest point and she has read many books that have made her fall in love with literature. She is also a self-motivated person, passionate and even to some extent very emotional. Her philosophy in life is that a person is what he or she chooses to be, and how each person chooses to be remembered is all up to him/her. Despite her introversion, her ability to make people at ease with her has made her circle of friends quite big. She is also a family person and a firm believer in God, whom she believes she is nothing without.

Amelia M.

Amelia M is a BA Honours student with the University of South Africa, and holds a BA degree in Public Adminstration and Political Science from the National University of Lesotho. Amelia lives in Khubetsoana, Maseru with her husband and child. She has no previous publications, but enjoys writing fiction and is currently writing an English novel that she hopes to publish in the near future.

Kaizer Matsumunyane

Kaizer Matsumunyane is a filmmaker, artist, and entrepreneur. He is also passionate about the art of craft beer. He has made projects in Lesotho, Japan, France, Hungary, Croatia, South Africa, Canada, Somali and Kenya. He studied film production in Cape Town, South Africa. He has produced directed and written documentaries, films, television series, music and corporate videos. Kaizer lectures about film and television at Limkokwing University of Creative Technology. Most of his work deals with social, political and economic issues. He is interested in stories of people trying to put pieces of themselves together every day in this indifferent world.

K. Phenduka

Katleho Phenduka was born in the district of Mohale's Hoek on the 16th June 1993. He is the first-born son of Tanki and 'Makatleho Phenduka. He spent most of his childhood at his maternal parents' house at Quthing Tele. He began his primary education at various schools which include Koung Ea Seaka Primary School and later completed his matric at Fezeka High School in Cape Town in 2010. Whilst there he joined the debate team and co-founded the school's poetry club in 2009 with Lwando Magwaqa. After high school he took a gap year and went to live with his uncle Mothofeela Lengoasa in Middleburg, Mpumalanga where he spent most of his time travelling and reading. In 2012 he got enrolled at the National University of Lesotho to pursue an LLB degree and he is in his fifth and final year of study. In varsity he is a member of the law society and he is the current judge president of the student judiciary committee, he is also involved in running charity projects, and career guidance in high schools. He lives with his younger brother Hlompho Phenduka and cousin Mats'oele Koloi at Roma.

Litšoanelo Nei

Litšoanelo Nei is a medical doctor with a passion for languages. She loves to read and occasionally write. She was one of the winners in the Ba re e ne re short story contest in 2015. She is also part of the duo that translated Ngugi wa Thiongo's story Ituīka Rīa Mūrūngarū: Kana Kīrīa Gītūmaga Andū Mathiī Marūngiī into Sesotho for the Jalada Translation issue.

Mojabeng Moholi

Mojabeng Anna Moholi is an introverted 22-year-old with a hyperactive imagination. She was born in the district of Maseru, in the suburban area of Hillsview. In her school years she attended Katleho Primary School, St James Anglican Primary School, Mabathoana High School and graduated at the National Health Training College with a diploma in Biomedical Sciences. Her first writing capabilities were expressed in primary school when she used escape being a social outcast through writing short fantasy stories. The idea to escape reality became merged with the ideology of wanting to express real stories with made up twists of science, technology, tradition and modern lifestyles to help people learn and relax.

One famous author once said to become a great author one has to be a great reader as well hence reading has become a great part of her life. Apart from using as a form of self-expression there are a few local writers and artists that influenced Mojabeng to pursue writing such people include Sejake Matsela, The Late Pearl Ocansey (Miss P) and her late grandfather Tseliso Moholi.

Nicole Tau

Nicole Tau is a fourth year student at the National University of Lesotho in the faculty of Humanities majoring in Literature and Linguistics. Born and bred in Russia until twelve years old, Nicole currently resides in Lesotho. Her known intense personality, assertiveness and love for public speaking encouraged

Nicole to participate in various debate competitions during her high school days. However, Nicole's love for writing and books has always prevailed since primary as she would entertain her friends with short written stories during their spare time. She only begun writing seriously at the university level but has not found a platform until now to fully express herself. Described as eccentric and a force to be reckoned with, Nicole has participated in more events and activities than she can personally count; literary and debate competitions in high school to volunteer jobs, boxing and adventurous jobs during her winter breaks. Thus, Nicole's biggest accomplishments are about personal fulfillment with regard to individual and intellectual growth. These days she spends time studying, writing, making handcrafts and building a hopefully prosperous future. Nicole Tau can be reached on facebook as Nyquolle Kim Lee or email taunicole@gmail.com.

Nthabiseng Lucy Kolobe

Lucy Kolobe was born on 22 May 1989 at Ha Matala Sekoting. She was raised by her grandparents. At age 18 she wrote her first book titled BOCHA which took almost 9 years before it could be published. In 2014 she worked in a small construction company called Bataung Chabeli Construction as a female supervisor. She also founded a community youth club which helps young children to know themselves through arts. In 2015 Lucy was one of the guests at the Ba re e ne re Literature Festival. Lucy is a self-taught writer and a high school graduate, but her love for writing says more. Her stories are non-fiction and a lot can be learned from them.

Ntimana Konyana – Semokonyane

As a lover of literature, Ntimana Konyana – Semokonyane is both diligent in her literary works and qualified in Literature in English teaching. Her love to write stories came as a rehabilitation practice from her life's social blackouts. Today, Ntimana has been able to shed her tears in her stories and grown into a vocational school facilitator in a local training institute. She started her manuscripts at the age of 17, when she left high school into tertiary. Many a time her write ups came as her way to vent and communicate her feelings and life experiences which she hardly shared with anyone.

Ntimana Konyana was born in Maseru on the 10th December, 1989. She fell in love with literature for the first time at 'Mabathoana High School and took it in further with her Bachelor's Degree in Education studied with NUL (2007 – 2011). She continues to write around her life. She is now married to Maripane Semokonyane, raising a son and working as a full-time as a Facilitating-Consultant in Occupational Safety, Health and Environmental Management.

Refiloe Mabejane

Refiloe Mabejane is a Mosotho writer of both fiction and non-fiction, living in Maseru. Her work appears in the anthologies The Bundle of Joy and Other Stories by Africa Book Club and To Kingdom Come: Voices Against Political Violence published by Onslaught Press Paris and London. Her short stories have also been featured in online publications Munyori Literary Journal and the Kalahari Review. She is a Trustee of the Family Art and Literacy Centre (FALC) where one of her main duties is to edit and facilitate publication of children's books for Basotho children. She has co-edited more than ten such books in the past eight years. Ms. Mabejane ultimately hopes to become a novelist, making a significant contribution to contemporary literature in Lesotho.

Rethabile Manong

Rethabile Manong is a Mosotho national, born some twenty-nine years ago in Teya-teyaneng. Rethabile trained as an English teacher, having studied at The National University of Lesotho and graduated with a B.Ed in English Language and Literature In English Teaching.

Rethabile got bitten by the writing-bug during the N.U.L days and since then has never stopped writing. Rethabile's collection boasts some 50+ poems, 1 complete novel and 10+ short stories. "Our Little Mystery" is by far my first literary work to be published. Though trained as a teacher, Rethabile is a natural-born philanthropist, community and youth mobilizer and girls' rights activist. Rethabile co-founded 'Mankabelane Theatre Group (N.U.L-2009) and is a Young African Leaders Initiative alumna. Their hobbies include dancing, acting, aerobics, travelling, watching movies, reading and of course writing. For Rethabile writing offers endless possibilities and a perfect space for a thousand thrills.

Selloane Tseka

Selloane Tseka is a young woman residing at Ha Thetsane. She was born of a Lesotho Evangelical Church priest Reverend Thobi Ramat'seliso Tseka and Maselloane Tseka at Matelile in the Mafeteng district. She attended Linareng Primary School at Tsikoane Leribe from 1997 to 2001 then attended Tsikoane High School where she finished her C.O.S.C in 2006. From there she studied Sociology and Social Anthropology at the National University of Lesotho where she graduated in 2011. Her life has been dedicated to voluntary work on a weekly basis, running a small business of her own and doing a few farming projects with her peers raising pigs and improved poultry. She also writes an inspirational column occasionally for Nameless, which is a youth digital magazine. Apart from her passion for writing, her hobbies include reading African literature, mainly novels by Chinua Achebe and Chimamanda Adiche. From there she enjoys writing romantic poetry for private consumption, for friends or working on her novel, which she hopes to publish soon. Her only sporting activities include jogging on warm Sunday mornings or taking long walks in the afternoon in the neighborhood of Ha Thetsane.

Tšeliso Monaheng

Tšeliso Monaheng is a freelance writer, photographer and film maker born and raised in Maseru. He currently lives and works in Johannesburg.

Khosi E. Rajeke

Khosi E. Rajeke is a winner of the Ba re e ne re *Freedom of Creative Expression* online writing competition. He works in collaboration with Khosiafines to create a synergy between fine art and the written word for the advancement of art and literature in Lesotho. Rajeke is also a Teaching Assistant and Special Education Needs Assistant at the National University of Lesotho.

Lerato Mensah-Aborampah

Lerato Mensah-Aborampah was born in 1997 in the district of Leribe and grew up there for a great part of her life with her mother and brother. The eighteen-year-old Mosotho girl now lives in Maseru, Lower Thamae. She is currently studying for her International Baccalaureate Diploma at Waterford

Kamhlaba United World College in Swaziland and will finish in 2017. She loves Chemistry and Literature and has recently taken a keen interest in Cultural Anthropology, which she studies at school. She has been passionate about writing since she was nine. She writes and occasionally performs her poetry. She also writes short stories (though most of these are not yet complete). More than mere literary pieces, she hopes for her short stories to amplify real and relatable issues evident in the everyday life of real people in society especially young people, with whom she shares most experiences. 'Young Basotho Writers' – a Facebook page she created, posts content that inspires aspiring young writers like herself. She feels very strongly about the growth and recognition of arts of all forms in Lesotho and aims to grow every day in her pursuit of writing impactful fiction.

Lipuo Motene

Lipuo Motene is a 28 year-old artist who works as a Creative Director at Kemet Designs and Creatives (Pty) Ltd. She holds a BA in English and Literature from the National University of Lesotho. Much of the inspiration in her writing journey is drawn from the human condition. She is a lover of African literature, hence her works are initiatives that highlight and celebrate the importance of Africanism. Among many African writers, she looks up to are renowned authors such as Chinweizu, Yaba Amgborale, Ngugi wa Thiongo, Cheikh Anta Diop, Fezekile Futhwa, Zakes Mda and Ayi Kwei Armah. These authors have a huge bearing on her works as they have impacted on her ideology and outlook on issues of identity and the much-revered Black Consciousness. Her hobbies are reading and writing. She writes critical essays, fiction and non-fiction as well as poetry. Some of her works have appeared in local newspapers and magazines. She is currently a student at the National University of Lesotho undergoing a Masters Degree in English Language and Linguistics.

M.V Darko

M.V Darko is the pen-name of Moso Victor Sematlane, an aspiring writer and screenwriter who lives in the small Mountain Kingdom of Lesotho. Though small, the country is bursting with big ideas and a creative energy that tends to foster expression in all forms, whether it's music, film or poetry. It's in this milieu that Moso has gravitated towards fiction, because he believes it has the power to create new realities and change lives. Moso writes because he has to; the alternative would be to go insane. A less dramatic reason however is that he's always loved books, and through his writing, wishes to make the world recognize them as the treasures they are as well. He's also an occasional slam-poet and devoted film-geek.

Liyah Jan

Liyah Jan, (born Mpolokeng Leteetee), is a highly driven singer-songwriter, with a great passion for reading and writing. Born and raised in Mohale's Hoek, she showed great interest in literature at a very early age, reading her mother's books and basically anything she laid her hands on. She went to Mohale's Hoek High School after finishing her primary school at St. Stephen's Primary School, then went to The National University of Lesotho where she immediately started working on her first novel, Kingdom In The Sky, after being persuaded by an old friend. The university is also where she accidentally fell prey to the literary world when her only option was literature when changing majors. After taking a class on Creative Writing, she knew she was on the right path. She now writes on a regular basis, with numerous unpublished short stories and two novels. She also works part time at the country's most popular radio station, The Ultimate Radio.
A mother to an amazing 8 year-old daughter, she also studies French, but her major dream is to attain the highest degree in literature and to have all her literary works published. For a short while, she was part of the writing team of the country's only soapie, Our Times, before returning to the university where she currently is.

Pontšo Mpholle

Ponts'o Mpholle is an avid observer, keen reader, enduring writer and overall lover of art with an unrelenting addiction to guava juice and an affinity for Malian music.

Tebby Letsie-Schoeman

Having had literature and creative writing forced on him at home during his primary school days (at the English Immersion School Project); Tebby Letsie-Schoeman (29) has not only become a traditional story-teller, but he is also a poet and a blogger. His blog *30 Random Days* saw thousands read and beg for more daily. Despite this history, Tebby however spent his early adult days in the fashion and pageantry industries then later retired into events management. During his varsity days at L'université Nationale du Lesotho, he co-founded a student magazine, *Varsity Breeze*, with his mates, which is where his writing talent was rediscovered and nurtured. Tebby has a very loud appearance and presence yet he is very shy and introverted. For the shy person that he is, his wit and articulation will leave your head in salt and pepper. Now based in Mohale's Hoek, Tebby has both his hands and feet dipped in hospitality, teaching and events management.

Wolf
Wolf (*Folane Makututsa*) grew up in Leribe, had a brief spell in Ankara studying engineering, adopted Taung as their second home two years ago and is now studying Law at the University of Cape Town. The places Wolf has lived in and the beautiful myriads met so far are what inspire Wolf to write. Wolf writes about all things beautiful - even the ugly. More of it is on Wolf's website, *www.beawolf.net.*

Mamoholi Mokhoro
Mamoholi Celestine Mokhoro is a 27 year-old Mosotho woman, married and has a daughter of three. She was born in the district of Thaba-Tseka in the year 1989. She lived there in the care of her grandparents then moved on to Leribe where she continued with her studies from a primary level to COSC. While in high school, her greater interest was with creative writing. She wrote a script based on the abuse of drugs and alcohol, and it gained her such publicity that she was invited to explore a filmed drama by a rising producer. Her favourite subject was Literature in English. Upon completion of her COSC she obtained an A grade in the very subject, inspiring her love for arts and culture. She has obtained a BA (Hons) in Broadcasting and Journalism at Limkokwing University of Creative Technology. She excelled in screen writing. She is now working on few writing projects as writing is her greatest passion. She views herself as a recognized author in the near future for both English and Sesotho books.

Acknowledgements

The Editors would like to thank Liepollo Rantekoa, the founder of the Ba re e ne re Literature Festival, for your continued inspiration. Your light shines on.

We share our appreciation for the Rantekoa family for being with us on the Ba re e ne re journey.

A great thanks goes as well to the additional members of the Ba re e ne re team – Lerato Molisana and Hlompho Letsie - who read and evaluated stories from the initial pool of submissions.

A huge debt of gratitude is owed to the supporters of our Indiegogo campaign who made this book possible. In particular, the following people made significant contributions:

- Lebohang Mochudi
- Rachel Zadok
- Robert Foord
- Rick Rosen, Heidi Nielsen and Max Rosen

Finally, in our promotion of Sesotho we like to create new words to show how dynamic the language can be. We define **Morepolli** as "someone who challenges power through creative expression." Our admiration and heartfelt thanks go to **Duduzile Mabaso** for being **Morepolli** in all that you do, especially in the realm of publishing.

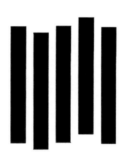

Made in United States
Cleveland, OH
12 December 2024

11710399R00114